WOMEN OF WINE COUNTRY

Murder & Mayhem

T Wells Brown

TITLE WOMEN OF WINE COUNTRY – MURDER & MAYHEM

Copyright © 2019 by T Wells Brown.

This book is a work of fiction. Names, characters, businesses, organizations, places, events and incidents either are the product of the author's imagination or are used fictitiously. Any resemblance to actual persons, living or dead, events, or locales is entirely coincidental.

For information contact :

Women of Wine Country

PO Box 132

Woodbridge Ca 95258

http://www.womenofwinecountry.com

Publisher : Women of Wine Country

Book and Cover design by Women of Wine Country

Author Photo Casey Evans Photography

Editors : Peggy Hamilton and Mary T Ward

Book Formating Women of Wine Country

ISBN: 9781082246081

First Edition : August 2019

10 9 8 7 6 5 4 3 2 1

*To the Love of My Life, your love and support allows
me to be a fearless woman.
If we only have twenty years left together - it isn't
enough time to tell
the world all the ways you make me a better human.
I will always love you, never doubt it.*

*To my mother, who didn't live long enough to see
her only daughter's dream come true.
Mom, if you can see me, I hope I've made you proud.
P.S. Say hi to Grandma for me!*

The Women of Wine Country Series has just begun!

Want more fun and excitement?
Watch for these titles releasing soon;
Lawyer & Liar – Sydney and Roman
Beauty & Betrayal – Jenna and Marcus

You'll need to stay current on all the Women of Wine shenanigans!

- ➢ Sign up for our email list at
  womenofwinecountry.com
- ➢ Follow us on Facebook Women of Wine Country group and like us on Facebook: @WomenofWineCountry Page for apparel and events in the Lodi Wine Appelation. See @authorwellsbrown for updates on the new series T Wells Brown is working on.
- ➢ Instagram @womenofwinecountry and @twellsbrown
- ➢ Pinterest: Women of Wine Country
- ➢ Twitter @twellsbrown
- ➢ Podcast Women of Wine Country on all the supporting PODCAST platforms

www.womenofwinecountry.com

Acknowledgements

First and Foremost, to my husband Donald, who teared up the first time I finally allowed him to read my work... and announced I was a writer, and the real push to publish began. That moment will forever be one of my all-time favorites.

To my beloved son Brandon, who always supports everything I do. You are the best partner I have ever had. It's been a long road, but you never lost faith in me ... even when I lost faith in myself. To my sweet son Richard, my DIL Merissa and my grandson Bryant; thank you for always supporting me.

To my sweet little ginger Divas who always love to hear my stories.

To my editors; Peggy and Mary, who agreed to edit my book even though all they do - all day long, is edit other people's work.

To Maria, who is my biggest cheerleader and confidant, who takes care of my home and family, so I have time to write. To Katie who was the first one to encourage me to write before anyone else. To

Samantha, who takes care of the business that pays the bills and keeps the lights on.

To my beta readers; I appreciate and love you all - to my two favorites, Aida and Kelly, thank you so much for taking time for my book and all the wonderful feedback.

Casey Evans Photography is my hero.

To my Women of Wine Country tribe - you hold me up when I am low. You all encouraged me when I felt down. The level of your excitement of this book ...almost matches mine. I won't ever forget your support.

Come join my tribe of wine guzzling bad-asses who give tirelessly to community and the charities that serve a common goal – a better quality of life for all.

We may drink more than most, party longer than many, may dance long after the music has stopped - but darling, it's all done with purpose and style.

-   Brandon Brown

Welcome

Thank you for your inquiry,

Women of Wine Country is a multi-dimensional organization devoted to the Lodi AVA, it's sub wine appellation's, businesses, communities and their charities.

We are dedicated to promoting women entrepreneurs and professionals, who live and operate businesses and/or charities in our wine region.

With 87 wineries in our appellation the opportunity to discover wonderful new wines and enjoy the winery's events are endless.

If you are interested in joining our Women of Wine Tasting tribe please check our website for the entry form, as well, you can check out our website and social media platforms for events happening in our beautiful wine country.

If you are a professional woman working in our wine region, please join our Women of Wine Country Networking Association. We are always eager to help promote other women operated businesses and professionals.

If you are a charity, and you believe your organization could benefit from our contributions, please contact our President Raquel Bellini of Bellini Estate and we will determine how we can best be of service.

We look forward to working with you and thank you for visiting our wine region.

Raquel Bellini
President
Bellini Estates
Women of Wine Country
www.womenofwinecountry.com

For more information on the fabulous wineries in our wine region,

Visit; www.lodiwine.com.

PROLOGUE

From inside the speeding car the only sound that could be heard was the pounding sheets of rain beating against the metal. There was zero visibility due to the windshield wipers inability to keep up with the torrential downpour. The frantic driver gripped the steering wheel, using it to pull himself closer to the windshield, as if that would allow him the ability to see the road ahead of him any clearer.

"Watch for falling rocks!" Antonio shouted to his passenger his eyes not leaving the windshield.

Panicked, he knew this road well enough to know; in a rain this hard, large rocks would skid off the side of the mountain and pummel the cars traveling the winding road below. He also knew the road well enough to know there were twists and turns everywhere, but not well enough to know exactly where all those twists and turns were.

"Slow down Antonio!" The female passenger screamed out in fear.

The pounding rain was so loud - even shouting she was difficult to hear.

"I can't! I've been pressing as hard as I can on the brakes, pumping the peddle and stomping down as hard as I can, and we just keep going faster!" Antonio shouted back. He knew they weren't going to make it. In the deepest part of his soul he knew this was going to be the last day on earth for him and his beautiful bride.

Their annual pre-harvest trip turned had into the last trip of their lives.

This wasn't how he wanted to end, not in this hard, unrelenting rain, not on this twisting, unforgiving road, with fear and panic so thick, he could smell, feel and taste it like a foul stench that permeated all of his senses.

This wasn't what he wanted for his amazing, full of life wife, who had given so much to live her life his way, to sacrifice so much to make him happy.

He wanted to walk ... just one more time...through their grape vineyards hand in hand.

One more time.

A desire he knew, tragically, was rapidly coming to an end.

Just one more time.

To watch a sunrise come up over their vibrant colorful vineyards.

To smell the rich pungent scent of his wine grapes fermenting.

Take in the delicious aroma of the freshly toasted oak barrels as they were unloaded for the new harvest.

Watch his beautiful wife walking towards him swinging her old tattered picnic basket, an old basket she refused to replace.... with his lunch packed inside, for a picnic in the middle of their dirty vineyard, and a brilliant smile on her face.

He wanted to grow old with her, hold her in his arms, stroke her thick soft hair while she rested her head on his chest.

But alas, he knew these desires were not to be fulfilled.

He knew, as the pit in his stomach grew, they were not going to survive this day. With every fiber of his being, he knew they were going to die. This would be their last day.

With his entire soul, all that he was, all she believed him to be... he silently swore to himself he wasn't going to let his beloved bride's last moments on earth be filled with fear and terror.

A calm tragic sadness washed over Antonio, as he said in a soft shout, "I love you my beautiful bride. I've never regretted one minute of our time together."

"Antonio..." she frantically screamed her reply, one hand stretched out to the dash and the other braced on the roof of the car.

"Baby listen to me, I am asking you to calm as much as you can and listen, I love you. I can't wait to see what God brings us to next."

"ANTONIO...." Was the last thing he heard as the car slid over the side of the mountainous road and tumbled several hundred feet to its final crumpled resting place at the base of the Feather River canyon.

He didn't hear his wife's reply as she whispered, "I will love you for eternity."

He didn't feel the car's metal crunch and cave in on them as it hit end to end, and then rolled side to side. Pieces of metal and plastic flying off the car during its descent.

He didn't hear the windows shattering or feel the glass blasting with force all around and over them as they tumbled down the side of the canyon wall.

He didn't feel the rain pouring in and pounding them as they came to rest near the bottom of the canyon.

He didn't hear or feel any of this. He was already dead from the seat belt failure, that allowed his head to hit the roof of the car, breaking his neck and killing him instantly on the very first tumble as they careened off the side of the mountain.

His wife, however, was not so fortunate. The angels looking down and guaranteeing Antonio's sudden death, did not do so well for her. She managed to stay alive, suffering...the metal painfully crushing in on her, the windows crashing in and blasting against the side of her face, neck and arm.

She felt every second, of every horrible, painful, tumble as she rolled down the side of the canyon. Until the end, when a tree drove through the windshield, pierced her chest and penetrated straight through her body, through her seat and finally stopping their descent near the bottom of the canyon, impaling her and the car, onto the tree.

One second, two, she felt it all, the pain, the horror, the grief knowing her life too was now over.

She struggled to breathe, to make sense of what had happened...and then, on her last shuddering breath, she was gone. Not experiencing a single moment of calm during this excruciating ending to reflect on her precious love or her life.

In her last moments, she felt pain, fright, and terrifying grief for her lost life. And in the final moment as her life flashed before her eyes, she took a small measure of comfort for a life well lived.

Headlights of the car that had been trailing the couple hit the curve where the now mangled vehicle had gone over the side of the canyon. The car stopped momentarily. The driver exited the vehicle in the pouring rain to look over the edge at the barely visible twisted metal below.

Taking out a phone, one picture, then two were snapped of the area where the car went over, and a final picture, of the best possible shot, of the wrecked car. Walked back to the running vehicle, climbed in and drove off never even considering calling it in for help.

Why would the driver?

Especially after all the trouble they had gone through to make the accident look just like that: an accident.

CHAPTER 1

The First Escape

I felt like an escapee.

I was running away… stealing away in the middle of the night from a bad place and heading (hopefully) into a better place.

I guess, in a way, I was.

Even though it wasn't night, and I was leaving the only real home I'd known for my entire life, potentially, never to return. If things went my way, that's what would happen. I still felt like I was getting away with something and from something.

You know how you hear those stories of people who lived their entire lives one way, and then something big happens that makes them re-evaluate everything they believed and knew to be true? Well, that is exactly what happened to me.

I sat in my spacious seat on the plane watching the other passengers board and was thankful for the first-class ticket my aunt's friend Sydney purchased for me. With so much weighing in on my shoulders, she was a blessing and luckily, also a force to be reckoned with.

There wasn't any way I could have afforded this extravagant ticket and her generosity was beyond anything I had ever known from anyone other than my loving aunt.

But that was my aunt Raquel's tribe, as they liked to call themselves: The Women of Wine Country. The ladies described themselves as a philanthropic club of do-gooders who saw to the needs of the under-served in their communities through wine tasting events.

That's right, wine tasting events.

HA!

They were more like a wine guzzling, bad-ass sisterhood that stuck to each other like gorilla glue.

I couldn't wait to see them.

Dealing with the sudden loss of my aunt was more than I was able to handle alone, and my momma was NOT helping, not one bit.

I had, of course, met them all, the Women of Wine Country tribe, during my summer visits when I was younger. And more recently, I heard about all of Sydney's scary over the top drama and their crazy goings on during my aunts and my weekly face-time chats.

Occasionally, they would drunk dial me (they called it tipsy time) but let's face it; those ladies could put away a few bottles of wine and then move on to the sparkly stuff without a thought – usually it was during the sparkly tipsy time I'd get drunk dialed or they would face-time me. They huddled around my aunt's phone, shouting into it, all at the same time, each one present trying to get their sage piece of advice to me over the voice of the other ladies who were shouting their sage advice, as well.

Usually, it was about how to deal with momma, but sometimes it was about why I was still single or if I had any prospects on the boyfriend scene. They would almost always finish up talking about my hair and trying to assure me of how pretty I was. I have really good hair.

I knew this because I got it from my momma, who had gotten it from her momma. My aunt Raquel also had really great hair 'cause she shared the same momma as my momma.

They were a glamorous, powerful, beautifully glorious group of amazing women who were absolutely bonkers, and I was flying, on a one-way first-class ticket, right into the middle of them.

And I couldn't wait to get there. To *them*.

I wish I could say I was returning to my aunt's winery and estate for a visit and to reconnect with her friends, but I wasn't. I was flying to my aunt's home because I was her only living heir, except momma, and she had left her and my uncle entire estate to me.

House, winery, vineyards, tasting room, catering & event business.... all of it was left to me.

Me!

I didn't know the first thing about how to do any of it.

Sure, I had spent most of my childhood summers with my momma at my aunt and uncle's, and later, when I was a teen, I spent the summers there without my momma, but I had always left right before the grapes would harvest and only helped in the cooking, serving and cleaning up part of the catering and event business.

With only a two-year business degree that took me three and a half years to obtain (due to my mothers' "episodes", which, truth be told, weren't even episodes but more like a way of life) I didn't feel equipped for the position I would need to take in order to make sure my aunt and uncles lifetime of work, everything they had worked so hard for, would survive their deaths.

That was another reason I was stressed. My momma and her sister, my aunt, did not get along; they were like oil and water. My aunt was a hardworking, smart, devoted wife and business owner, who had a ton of friends and took care of her community.

My mother was a quiet, reserved, judgmental woman when she was sober....and a selfish, mean, nasty, loud, opinionated drunk.

Unfortunately, she preferred to stay drunk most of the time. She not only didn't care about her community, mostly she held animosity towards it and resented everyone who lived in it.

My aunt and my momma's falling out happened the last time we went to spend the summer in California together. I was fifteen and my mother had started drinking on the plane and stayed drunk the entire trip, which meant I was her prime target of discourse.

My uncle first took notice the second day of our visit and tried to stick up for me, but when things escalated quickly, my aunt had to step in and rescue my uncle. It was downhill from there. The next two months were a cycle of momma getting drunk, me being a target for her spitefulness and my aunt and or uncle stepping in. It usually ended with a huge fight. The fight then turned into an excuse to drink until she passed out and would wake up sometime the next day, not remembering any of it.

Or so she said.

The process would start all over again the next morning when she started drinking mimosas. The winery was a bad place for her. She had more alcohol at her disposal than she knew what to do with, and let me tell you, she tried, she tried really hard, to consume as much as she possibly could.

My poor aunt, who, no matter how hard she worked, could not get my mother to see reason. She tried several times into talking my momma into staying with them and getting some kind of treatment. Back then, I didn't really understand how serious it was or would turn out to be – I was only fifteen. But momma refused and always turned every drunken episode into another bigger fight and would blame the fight on anyone but herself.

That was the last trip my mother made with me to California. After that I went on my summer break alone and would always have a huge fight with her before leaving and a huge fight when I got home. After four years in a row of doing this, I simply stopped going.

Anyway, when I made that decision, I thought I would be in college full time and wouldn't be able to make the long vacations. My aunt and uncle would fly in to see me for a few days each year around my birthday, and then they would have to head back to take care of business.

Let's just say without my aunt and uncle, I would have had a terrible life. With them, I had a bearable life. If we had lived closer to them, I could have spent more time in their company, and I would have been able to complete a four-year college degree and possibly had a real career.

That wasn't my reality though. I had to finish taking my courses online at night just to get the two-year degree. My momma's drunken state escalated each time I got close to reaching any sort of milestone.

Because of that, she never learned I finished the two-year degree. She thinks I never finished college, which she throws in my face as often as she possibly can. I keep that real close to the vest. If she ever found out I finished even my meager two-year degree behind her back, there would be serious hell to pay, and I just wasn't up to deal with that level of torment.

Especially now…. without my aunt around to have my back, or even to commiserate with.

Until three days ago, I worked as an office assistant for a construction company husband and wife team. It paid the bills, barely, but they understood my situation and not only gave me the time I often needed to manage her episodes, but they helped me when they could. During the holidays, they would check on me to make sure I had a way to celebrate and wasn't left alone. They were nice and I would miss them. They even drove me to the airport and sent me off with tears and a promised to stay in touch and check in on momma.

Several times, I tried talking to my momma about her drinking and these discussions segued into some of the worst fights and verbal and physical abuse I had ever received from her. After the last attempt, I just didn't have it in me to bring it up again.

She flitted through life on a whim (hers) and a prayer (mine) and went through jobs like water went through a screen. My worst fear was if I ever left her, she would end up homeless, in the hospital, or in jail. No matter how much she upset me, she was still my momma and I wasn't having any of it. I stayed with her, in the same small house my aunt and uncle had bought us when I was little and worked and paid the bills and picked her drunk butt up and put her to bed most nights.

But that was all about to change.

Occasionally, I would get a brief reprieve when she would start dating someone and during those times, she would really clean up her act. But she couldn't keep it up for long and sooner or later she would end up showing her true colors and it would always cost her the guy.

See, when I say my momma was a mean nasty drunk, that's me sugar -coating the situation. That woman was downright vicious. And once she set her eye on you that was it, and there was not one dang thing you could do to shake her until she tore you down to the level, she felt you deserved to be.

Thus, she went through a lot of men.

Luckily, we lived right outside of Houston, so she had a huge selection of men to go through and as of yet, hadn't managed to go through them all.

With all that said, I was fortunate to be leaving during a time when momma was dating someone new and was on her best behavior. The fact that her sister had just died gave her something to use to milk all the sympathy out of the poor guy she could, and probably buy her some time to atone for her crappy behavior. He would chalk it up to grief and it might be a while before he realized this was how she was and there wasn't goin' to be another normal she would go back to.

I did, however, make sure the man she was dating, Mark, knew my number and how to get ahold of me, just in case.

Tragically, my momma attracted nice guys who wanted to take care of her and help fix her; they were all the hero types who loved to sweep my poor weak momma off her feet.

Then, after a spell, they would come to find my momma was not only - not weak, she was as mean as a starving feral cat, and they would hightail it outta our lives like their britches were on fire.

I stretched my legs out and marveled at the roominess of the leg area and at the comfort this seat afforded me. I thought back to all the times I'd flown to see my aunt in the cramped normal airline seats. This was so much better.

See, my momma, my aunt Raquel and I were tallish; five feet ten inches and all of us looked alike. Momma and aunt Raquel were twins. I looked like they probably did when they were my age. We all were kind of curvy: big boobs, big butts, long legs with thick thighs with a little buddha belly. Each of us had long dark wavy/curly thick soft hair that naturally highlighted to a burnished copper when in the sun for a few hours. We have big round light brown eyes, with long thick lashes.

I learned we were attractive at a very early age because, while traveling together when I was younger, we were treated a certain way by everyone, men and women alike, and of course, in my later years I learned we were attractive in the usual ways.

Men loved us, then didn't. Women were wary of us and kept us at arm's length.

Except my aunt's wine tribe gals. They just loved us.

Now normally, you think twins are close. I guess when they were little, the two of them had been, they knew what each other was thinking, had a secret language and all.

But once my momma discovered boys and alcohol, things changed dramatically. My understanding was things started going south for my aunt when momma got really jealous of anyone who would meet her sister and make a big fuss, embarrassing my aunt. This usually made momma look small and petty. I guess maybe that's when she started drowning her sorrows in a bottle, leading to a lifetime of drowning all her many sorrows, in as many bottles as she could get her hands on.

Momma was also really pissed that Sydney only sent me a ticket, and told my mom she wasn't welcome, nor was she inheriting anything.

"Not. One. Penny" were Sydney's exact words. Although miles separated my aunt and Sydney for a few years, they talked almost daily, between that and social media, they shared everything.

To put it mildly...this information did not go over well. But there wasn't anything momma could do about it. Sydney was the executor of the will and even though I only remember meeting Sydney when I was little, my momma knew her, and knew her well enough to be cautious of her.

My momma's last words to me as I was walking out the door was, "Well, we'll just see about this, now won't we?" I'm not going to lie – the words, and the way in which they were spoken, in her deep southern drawl, scared the heck outta me and I hightailed my rear end outta there as quick as I could. I think the only saving grace was my momma and her new guy were just home from a short trip they had taken to California and momma wasn't in a big hurry to get back on a plane right away.

I was sure that night was going to be a real humdinger and for once, I was not going to be around with a big neon target on my forehead. Let the new guy deal with her. My entire life had been dedicated to her and her episodes and I'd had enough.

Any and every opportunity to advance myself, and my life, from school, to jobs, to boyfriends, to friends, to apartments, she would work, and scheme, and make scenes, and lie until I was forced back to her home. Under her rules, her abuse and I gotta tell ya, I was damn sick and tired of it. I knew at this point in my life, it was her or me. For the first time, I was choosing me.

I needed some peace in my life, or I was going to end up just as nutty as she was. I loved my momma, that went without saying. But I needed some space from her, and I was taking it.

The plane landed with a jolt at the Sacramento airport, "Ladies and Gentlemen please remain seated until we've taxied to our gate. Once again, thank you for flying with us today. On behalf of our crew we welcome you to Sacramento, California's state capitol."

Disembarking was easy from the first-class section. This was a great way to fly. I wasn't under any illusion I'd ever be able to have this experience again; I mean seriously first class, so I was very appreciative of all the perks it offered.

Since I had packed most of my meager belongings, I was lugging a carry on around with me, and had two suitcases to collect. I left the secured area, hopped on the transport train, and headed towards the baggage claim area which was located on the first floor. The bright warm sun shining through the glass walls was such a weird contrast to the dark mood that seemed to have overcome me.

My mind kept going back to the one unchangeable fact: my aunt was gone.

She was the one person I took comfort in. If it all fell apart, she would be there to catch me unconditionally and completely. She was the safety net that allowed me the tolerance to deal with momma; she was the solid presence that kept me from despair.

Now that security was gone and I was feeling like there was not any firm ground under my feet, and there might never be again.

With those dark thoughts looming, I was unprepared for what was waiting for me as I descended the escalator leading to the baggage claim.

CHAPTER 2

Meet the Tribe

They were there.

All of *them*.

My aunt's friends from her Women of Wine Country tribe were there waiting for me.

Each, and every one.

Sydney, I recognized right away from our face-time chats. She had shoulder length dark brown hair, with the front sides longer than the back and the ends in the front were blonde. She was shorter than I, cute and petite, with big round sage green eyes and olive completion. With her high, sharp cheek bones and mouth covered in a dark red lipstick, her appearance even more striking in person than her pictures and face-time showed. She was a kick ass lawyer who had been through hell and was now back. She was holding a carrier that I already knew held Agatha, Sydney's feline sidekick, a gray tabby, who was better traveled than most of the people at the airport.

Jenna was easy to pick out: I'd seen her transformation since her divorce through social media, where she had a big following, as well as my aunts face-time chats. She was stunning and heads turned everywhere she went. She had long silver blonde hair, bright green eyes with long thick black lashes and a small athletic build. Even with all that, what really made people take notice was her dress and mannerisms. She was, without a doubt, everything we all wanted to be in beauty, and all the things we hoped we would get out of our beauty products. Jenna was a shrewd businesswoman who claimed her superpower was... being underestimated.

Becca, in her trademark cowgirl boots; she'd paired with a light pink sundress, was one of those lucky gals who is naturally blessed with super healthy tanned skin and was toned from working on her ranch. Becca also had the best head of hair, a riot of light and medium-brown curls that cascaded to the middle of her back. She had the brightest blue eyes I had ever seen, a color that did not come through in its intensity on social media or the face-time chats. Also, smart people did not want to be on the bad side of this woman. She would kick anyone's butt without a thought.

Terra, the tallest and thinnest of them all, was standing towards the back of the group with her black, shiny, teased shoulder length hair. Her big black almond shaped eyes stood out beautifully against her porcelain skin. She was what we call in the south "uppity", but she had a heart of gold and was one of my aunt's dearest friends.

Juliette and Stella, sisters who looked so much alike you'd think they were twins, instead of the two-year age difference they had. The biggest physical difference about them was Juliette's hair was a full head of untamable dark red curls that fell in a mass of perfect ringlets almost to her rear, and Stella's long red hair was stick straight with blonde ends. They're curvy gals with tiny waists who loved to run, hike, kayak and do all things outdoors. Both were so well educated my aunt Raquel and her tribe stopped counting their degrees and academic accomplishments years ago.

Francesca, I noticed, was the only one who hadn't come. Sydney had brought me up to date on her sad situation when we had spoken, so I knew she was sitting by her husband's side during his hospice care.

That thought brought me back around to where I was now. The ground started to become firm under my feet once again, with each step bringing me closer to the women. My foothold becoming more solid.

Walking as fast as I could in their direction, all my fears and sadness bubbled up and I burst out crying, overcome with grief, relief and just plain being scared.

The building emotions made me walk faster and faster, until I was clumsily jogging, with my ginormous carry-on bag, the last few feet to them.

Maybe I wouldn't be as alone as I thought. Maybe, just maybe, my aunt had left me in the hands of people who would be able to help hold me up.

But of course, I should have known she would. She never let me down, not once in all my years. I let her down plenty, especially when it came to momma - but she never, not once, let me down. It seemed even death wouldn't keep her from taking care of me, seeing me through making sure I was okay, cared for, looked after and loved. Her and my uncle's love was the only real love I'd ever known that didn't come with terms, conditions and drama that would eventually result in heart break.

When they saw me and my reaction to them, they all, in unison, started walking quickly to me, and when I started jogging, they did too...towards me. As a group they all jogged, arms outstretched. They were all in varying degrees of crying, and when we finally came together, we pulled each other in for a big sobbing huddle of grief-stricken women.

In that moment, holding onto each other was all we had, all we knew, and all that mattered.

The crying, female "grief - huddle" lasted only a few minutes, because one of the two men who had accompanied the group reached in, pulled me out of the middle of the ladies and asked me, "Do you think you can identify your bags for us? Unless you want them to get sent back to Texas."

This was said to me by the manliest man I had ever seen in my ever-loving life and I was from Texas!

He was hanging onto my arm, looking at me.

I looked down at his large hand on my arm and back up to his handsome face.

This guy was super tall, and I was tall! He was taller – way taller than me. He had a dark olive complexion, light gray eyes and short black hair; he looked like he was Mediterranean, Greek maybe. I dunno, it didn't matter, cause *Jumpin' Jezebel's* he was fine!

He'd manage to shake me out of my grief. Honestly, I'd never been this close to such a fine specimen of man before and I didn't know, if in my grief, I was seeing things, so I shook my head to clear my befuddled brain.

"No?" He asked me in his deep voice, his light eyes going wide.

Oh shoot! He thought I was saying no about the...wait, what did he ask me again?

"Oh, knock it off, Cabe. Honey, wipe your eyes and let's go find your suitcases ok?" Sydney handed me a tissue, interlocked her arm with mine, and together we started walking towards the baggage carousels, with the sniffling lady group following closely behind us.

"Who's that guy?" I whispered to Sydney.

"That's Cabe. Pretty isn't he?"

"Yeah, that's putting it mildly," I said looking back over my shoulder, to see he was right on our heels, was looking at my rear, and could hear everything we said.

I flushed.

His eyes met mine and he smirked.

Jumpin' Jezebels!

That was embarrassing!

After collecting my bags, we made it out of the terminal and piled into the SUV's they'd brought to pick me up.

The car ride wasn't bad at all, the ladies talked back and forth the entire time, and before I knew it, we made the turn that led to my aunt and uncles home Bellini Estates. Turning off the long road onto the estate was emotional. I'd never, not once dreamed I'd be returning without Raquel and Antonio here to greet me.

The house they'd lived in sat directly across the brick courtyard from the winery, event hall and tasting rooms, and was surrounded by acres of my uncle Antonio's beloved vintage grape vines.

The estate was just as I remembered it, if not more beautiful. I'd always fantasized about living there and how happy I'd be if this was my home. I guess soon, I was going to find out if that was going to be a reality or not.

Looking around, I felt a heaviness that seemed to hang over the estate. It was sad, but somehow comforting to be here, like I could possibly recapture some of the time I had lost with Raquel and Antonio.

The old buildings were reconstructed on the inside, but still had the amazing old clinker brick exteriors. All four three-story buildings faced the giant brick courtyard, and in the center, sat a magnificent bronzed water fountain. It was cast from a huge old gnarled grape vine, with a giant trunk, and water running down all of its twisted fingers into the shallow pool below. My uncle Antonio had the sculpture cast from one of his oldest vines, and after my aunt, this was his pride and joy.

The sound of the water fountain was soothing and added an element of calmness to the brick courtyard.

Four three-story high square white columns graced each entry of the four buildings. Huge old cathedral double doors with black iron fittings, each slightly different than the other, graced each doorway. The winery, the event hall, Raquel and Antonio's home, and the tasting rooms faced the brick courtyard. The courtyard wasn't just pretty but functional with cast iron bistro tables and chairs placed around the fountain. The buildings and their carefully preserved architecture were amazing; and the site of many weddings, as well as other formal and causal events.

There really wasn't anything like it at any of the other eighty plus wineries in the region. Most of the Lodi Wine Appellation wineries had gone with the natural stone and stucco look so prevalent with the Mediterranean style, or the modern updated minimalist look, but not my aunt and uncle.

No.

They maintained the look of the region when the vines had first been planted over one hundred and fifty years ago. This much I knew from all the long walks with my uncle Antonio. The buildings, just like the vineyard, had been creatively updated with all the newest technology and conveniences that they could afford, without disturbing the old bones and architectural features, those were lovingly kept intact.

This made the Bellini Estate and Winery unique to the region.

Come to think of it, now that I was back here at this beautifully rustic, yet majestic winery estate, a lot of what my uncle had taught me was starting to come back.

My aunt Raquel's house was a clinker brick home, the biggest home I'd ever been in, with six bedrooms, seven bathrooms and the entire third floor that was the master suite. Both her home and the event hall had gleaming efficient commercial kitchens with white cabinets and stainless-steel counters. My aunt Raquel loved to cook more than almost anything. She cooked for all the events at the winery, and every holiday she would put on an amazing feast in her event hall where everyone was invited.

With a heavy heart, the realization hit me, I would never sit at one of her beautiful tables or enjoy one of her fantastic meals again. I'd never get to make up for the time I'd missed with them. I had chosen to appease my momma, rather than spend time with the two people who probably loved me most in the world. There was a huge ball of guilt sitting square in the center of my chest, and it was settling in to stay a while. I deserved to feel every miserable moment of it. I should have been a better niece to them both. I should have put them first and my momma's manipulative ways second.

It turned out Sydney was staying with me at Bellini for a while; she flew in the day before. She was having some weird silent argument or fight, or something with the other man who came to the airport. His name was Roman, and he was hot – like super-hot – like HOT! Hot! Here in wine country, all the men must be drinking the hot guy water, and it was working!

Hot guy Cabe and his super hunky side kick Roman took my bags up to one of the guest rooms on the second floor. I followed the ladies into the kitchen to help with lunch preparations.

Before I could figure out what I needed to do to help, Sidney pulled me aside and announced to the room that we were going to take a few moments to talk business.

My aunt Raquel's friend Jenna said, "Are you sure now is the time?"

"She needs to know where she stands and the plans we've made so far before someone else tells her and gets it wrong or freaks her out." Sydney replied.

Well shoot.

"Now I *am* freaking out. Let's have this talk so we can come back here and eat with them, ok?" I said.

"Come on Bella," Sydney replied softly, taking my hand and leading me to the library just off the dining room. My aunt used to call me Bella when I was younger but had stopped the last time I visited with my momma, because momma used the affectionate nickname to mock me.

Sydney who had been out of the country these last six years, wouldn't know that, or at least wouldn't know it was a painful reminder, or so I thought.

"My aunt stopped calling me Bella when I was fifteen," I told her.

"I know she did; she told me. I think its bullshit and I think the reason why was bullshit, so I am going to keep her endearment alive and continue to use it." She stopped walking and turned to me, "Unless of course, it hurts you," she finished softly.

With tears in my eyes I replied quietly, "I like it." And gently squeezed her forearm.

Settling into my aunts cozy overstuffed chairs in her library, Sydney wasted no time getting straight to the point and laid it all out for me.

"Bella, Raquel and Antonio were very careful how they formed their estate and wishes. You are their heir and they left the bulk of their estate to you; however, they left provisions and requirements for others too."

"Okay. What does that mean exactly?" I asked, not following.

"Well, first off; they retained me to be executor of the estate for this first year, with the idea that you would be settled in fully, but they also left provisions for me to extend for a second year in case you needed me. This would be decided by you. I don't have a say after this first year. Does that make sense?"

"Yes. I really appreciate your help, Sydney, and I know how much my aunt and uncle trust you." We both went still at my comment, realizing I was talking as if they were still alive.

I felt a single tear roll down my cheek. "I'm sorry," I hiccupped.

Sydney watched me closely for a few minutes, letting me calm myself, and then said, "The reading of the will is the day after the funeral here at the house. There are a few charities and loyal employees they have made provisions for, and some other people named in the will, and they will all be here as well. But you should know beforehand, it would be a good idea to start securing certain things, so we don't lose footing. Things are a little rocky on the homestead."

"What things? What do you mean rocky?" I asked.

"Raquel and I talked almost daily and sometimes several times a day. She was my best friend..." Sydney stopped talking and looked down at her hands resting in her lap. Taking a deep breath, she continued, "but Raquel and Antonio were also my clients, and they were having issues with, well primarily, two of the larger wineries. We are heading into harvest and crush, this year the old vine fruit was sold to a different winemaker than previous years. I negotiated the deal for the benefit of Bellini Estate. The negotiations alone caused quite a commotion with the two wineries that had been receiving the fruit, and under paying your uncle." She went on, "Three years ago, I encouraged and subsequently strong armed your uncle into having his old vines DNA tested at UC Davis. See, your uncle has the three old vine vineyards, which surround the estate. You already know those are Zinfandel. He also has the 'younger' vines he planted when he bought up the land adjacent to the estate, and across the street. Now they are well over twenty years old, but they are not considered old vine yet. Anyway, the two old zin vineyards are doing well, nothing changed with those. However, the DNA results came back and the seventy-five acres of old vines we originally thought were Black Malvoisie, turned out to be what we believe to be the world's oldest surviving Cinsault Vineyard."

She stopped talking and looked to me expectantly, as if I had understood one thing she'd said.

"I don't understand any of what you just said Sydney. You're gonna have to break it down for me."

"Okay. In a nutshell, Raquel and Antonio, have been battling two of the region's largest wineries for the Cinsault fruit. They have been very aggressive in their pursuits and the winery has even experienced some small bits of vandalism since the DNA discovery. Your uncle was working with Cabe to secure the old vines and set up monitoring in the vineyards before they died. Since I negotiated this last deal for the Bellini Estate with the new buyer, things began to escalate." She stopped talking and with her forehead furrowed she said, "The deal is done, but I had just gotten it done, and since I wasn't handling things here but from France no one knew who the buyer was or if the deal was signed." saying under her breath to herself, "I need to let Cabe know this."

"So, what you're telling me is that Antonio had decided to sell his oldest grapes to a new buyer for more money and the old buyers got pissed?"

Sydney looked at me with a small smile, "Yes, that is correct."

"Well, if the deal was already done what can the old buyers do about it?" I asked.

"Nothing, but they don't know that because they didn't know the deal was finished. Also, one of the wineries had award winning wines based on Antonio's crop."

"So, they might think they still have a hand to play? And they're desperate?" I asked.

"Yes, and my concern is they might approach you after the reading of the will to try and negotiate the fruit."

"The fruit?"

"Yes, that's what they call the grapes."

"Oh. Okay." Grapes were fruit, so that made sense.

"The vineyards all of them, the estate, the equipment and everything Raquel and Antonio hold dearest are mostly yours now. Like I said before, they made provisions for a few charities and loyal employees, which was very generous of them. But you are left with the bulk of the estate and enough operating capital, after your inheritance taxes, to get you through at least five harvests if you operated at a no gain status. That's not what we want to see happen, but your aunt and uncle were extremely smart businesspeople and knew God and Mother Nature had too big of a say in their industry not to have a backup plan. Antonio being Antonio, of course, had a back up to his back up. No one knows this, and not very many businesses operate this way, but your uncle comes from an old established wine making family in Italy and his ancestors had been through so much throughout the numerous generations, he brought their preparedness with him when he came here and he has extended you with this too."

"So, if I can't make the winery any money in the next five years I will be in trouble?" I asked.

"Well, you have the estate and the catering business your aunt ran. That was very successful as well, so you could technically support yourself and the estate with that, but you would not be able to support the wine making at a loss and everything else unless you made some changes to the catering model Raquel had in place."

"Like what changes?" I asked.

41

"Raquel only catered events here at the winery. That was plenty for her; she kept busy all year. But let's say, if you were to hire a bakery chef and made pastries and specialty cakes to be used here and sold elsewhere, could be another revenue stream and one Raquel was talking to me about because she has the two commercial kitchens, and she wasn't keeping them both busy. Also, you could cater events not held here at the winery. Raquel wasn't interested in this, but you could view it as a 'worst-case scenario' type of revenue stream we might be able to tap into."

She continued on, "You might also consider keeping the wine tasting rooms open longer and schedule musicians to help draw people here. You could set up the main house as a B&B. Steve and Allistor won't be happy, but if you're doing that, things have really taken a turn and I'm sure we could work something out."

Steve and Allistor were the only male members of the Women of Wine Country tribe; neither of them drank a lick of alcohol. Steve, due to him being a recovered alcoholic and diabetic. Allistor was so devoted to his Baptist upbringing and was unbelievably innocent in all things altering his state of being. This meant they made perfect designated drivers.

They were a husband/husband team that worked diligently at the animal rescue my aunt's Women of Wine Country tribe supported. The couple owned an old Victorian down the road from my aunt and uncle's estate and had lovingly restored it to its original grandeur, all the while updating the amenities. They'd turned it into a B&B that offered continental breakfasts and winery tours in their huge suburban with their B&B logo on the doors.

Steve was a retired correctional officer and was one big hunk of a man. He suffered from diabetes and had recently had an infection that cost him his left foot and lower leg. My aunt said he bounced right back and was so busy living the good life, happy just to be alive, he didn't let it slow him down in the least.

Allistor, however, did not fare as well, Allistor was so sensitive to his husband's amputation they jokingly referred to it as "Al's amputation." Allistor found no humor in this and really didn't appreciate being called 'Al'.

Steve was a big handsome white guy, with light brown hair and dark brown eyes. He'd been married once to a woman for several years who was still his friend and visited the couple often. He didn't come out until he was in his forties and from the way he tells it, it was not a pleasant experience.

Allistor was a beautiful half black half Greek GOD of a man, with beautiful dark skin, dark hair and brilliant light green eyes. He had never been with a woman romantically, and never had to come out because he was never in. Raised by his mom and four older sisters; he grew up in a Baptist church (a church he still attended) that seemed to uphold the idea that we are all God's children and Allistor was perfect just the way he was.

Which he was. He had recently retired from the
hospitality industry, so the B&B was a perfect fit for
them both.

They were often part of the Tipsy Time facetime
chats I would come to cherish over the last few years,
and often they would be the only people I could
understand because they would be the only ones not
shouting at the phone. My aunt loved these two men
and counted them as part of her family. They spent
holidays together and relied on each other like family
does and were for all intents and purposes...you
guessed it; family.

"Where are Steve and Allistor?"

"They're housing several of the out of town people
who came in for the funeral and they also had to pick
Kathy up from the airport." Kathy was Steve's ex, who
also knew my aunt and uncle from her regular stays at
the B&B.

"Another thing, as you well know, the house you
and your mom live in is yours. It's been in a trust for
you since it was purchased, and based on the
instructions of the trust, if you aren't living in the home,
it's to be sold and the monies then handed over to you.
However, I might suggest you consider giving or renting
the home to your mother to keep her there. I don't think
it's a good idea, with all you have to learn the next
couple of years, to let her be a disruption. It's only going
to make things harder on you."

I sat there in shock, looking at Sydney. "What do you mean the house is in a trust for me? And that if I'm not living there it's to be sold?"

"You didn't know?"

Shaking my head, no, I said, "Tell me. Tell me right now." The blood was pumping so hard through my head I could hear and feel the pulsation.

"When your aunt bought the house, she told your mother as soon as you moved out, the house would be sold, and you'd get the money for college or whatever you needed it for. And you are saying you didn't know?"

Oh my God. I couldn't breathe. I gripped the armrests of the chair I was sitting in and sat straight, my back ramrod and said, "are you saying the reason my mom got me kicked out of every house and apartment I ever moved to - and the reason I had to secretly finish college without her knowing - is because SHE WOULD LOSE THE HOUSE!?" I screeched.

All this time I thought my mom was so dysfunctional and needy because of her alcoholic ways that she couldn't stand her life without me. But it wasn't that at all; she literally ruined anytime I tried to move forward so she could live rent free in my house. She used to say to me all the time "My house. My rules." Now, I know that's a typical normal parent thing to say, but it wasn't her house and her only rules were based on her own selfish needs.

Jumpin' Jezebels!

Now I was PISSED!

"THAT FUCKING BITCH!!!" I shouted at the top of my lungs, shoving to my feet, causing Sydney to jump in her seat. Right then Cabe ran into the room, stopping just inside the doorway looking around, braced and ready to battle.

I gotta say, it completely stole the edge of my outrage. He was that hot. Running in to do battle! Even hotter.

"What the fuck?" He kind of yelled.

"Isabella just learned some disturbing news Cabe, and you might want to brace yourself, because there's going to be a lot of female outbursts and crying and maybe some drunkenness happening before the week is out." Sydney scolded him.

"Fuck me," he grumbled in his deep voice as he spun on his heel and walked back out the way he'd come in.

"Cabe and Antonio were extremely close; no one else knows this winery like Cabe. Try to be patient with him, okay?" Sydney asked me, patting my hand.

Since his presence had derailed some of my anger because he really was that handsome, I shook my head and asked Sydney, "Anything else I should know before I eat and take a shower?"

"Two things. One: if you are going to keep this winery you are going to have to learn to drink wine, at least taste it and know what it is you are tasting."

"I don't..."

She interrupted me, "I know you don't drink, and I know it's because of growing up with an alcoholic mother. But this is different and you're going to have to get your head around it. If you can't, you might as well figure out how to sell off the winery portion of the business. You can still grow grapes, but you can't be a boutique winery owner who doesn't know her wines. Two: I have a letter for you. Raquel left all of the truly important people in her life letters. I am handing them out before the funeral except yours. I have yours and I want you to take it now, but honey, I think you should tuck it away somewhere safe and let all of this rest for a while, before reading it. Okay?"

Well, wasn't that just perfect.

CHAPTER 3

A Dark Day

The funeral was a devastating affair, despite the elegant surroundings, beautiful and beautifully dressed people in full attendance. Every corner of the church packed to standing room only.

The Women of Wine Country legion was vast. The sisterhood extended to all areas of the world where wine was made, and grapes were grown. My Aunt Raquel being the president of her chapter meant all the members who were physically able to attend, did.

This was a testimony to my wonderful Aunt Raquel and Uncle Antonio, their devotion not only to friends, but to their community as well. Both were well known for all of their good works; that also meant the charities in the area knew they were giving, generous and kind. If they couldn't help with a specific charity, they would find someone who would. This was apparent based on the number of people who showed up and grieved for the devastating loss of two amazing people.

The two deep burgundy caskets at the front of the church, covered in a base of magnolia leaves and branches, and topped with beautifully arranged pale pink and white flowers of every variety, were stunning. My aunt had planned her and my uncle's funerals three years previously when she updated their wills, never dreaming both of them would be buried together. Her provisions had counted on and included one of them still being alive – now those duties fell to Sydney and me.

Sydney, yes. I could understand her. She was strong, educated and so together. She made sense.

Me?

I, who couldn't stop crying. My eyes puffy and red.

With all the crying I wouldn't be able to keep any makeup on, so the only thing I could do was keep my lips coated with deep red lipstick and not worry about any other makeup. I wasn't trying to impress anyone anyway.

My aunt's tribe had shown up earlier that day with clothes, shoes, hats, gloves, bags and all things needed to get the whole tribe ready for the funeral together. During our pre-funeral preparations, the group cried, hugged and carried on, alternating between drinking a variety of white wines and coffee and helping each other get dressed.

It was crowded and busy and perfect. They wanted to give my Aunt Raquel and Uncle Antonio the sendoff they deserved, and that was going to be nothing but the absolute best.

Jenna brought over outfits for me to try on, beautifully made, soft and perfect for my voluptuous shape. The black pencil skirt I chose fell just below my knees, with a gold zipper at the back that ran from the bottom of the skirt all the way up to the waist of the skirt, and girl. It fit like a glove, made of some kind of perfect stretchy material that flattened my little tummy and hugged my big butt. The top was a very simple black sheer capped sleeve with built in camisole, a little lose fitting and looked beautiful tucked into the skirt.

My shoes were sweet: black shiny patent leather pumps with thick heels and a platform peekaboo toe. They had little golden studs running up the back of the heel and up the back of the shoe. My bag was a darling little black patent leather clutch with a gold chain for the shoulder strap; it matched the shoes, gold studs and all. I'd never worn anything so glamorous and it was a real shame, but also fitting, that it would all be for Raquel – even though she wouldn't be able to see me wearing it. This thought brought on a whole new round of tears.

I'd decided against wearing any jewelry. I didn't have much anyway.

Once we were all ready, the tribe as a beautifully dressed black clad group, descended upon me and presented me with a full, sparkling, beautiful charm bracelet that I knew like I knew the back of my hand. I knew it because it was Raquel's. It was the charm bracelet all the Women of Wine Country wore with pride. They added their charms as they had adventures together. Each charm meant something special for each woman. No two bracelets were exactly the same, but all of them held many of the same charms. Of course, they had wine charms, grape charms, wine glasses, champagne glasses, little shoes and handbags, and paw prints with glittering stones, just to name a few.

However, Raquel's charm bracelet held a custom piece none of the others had, and I knew it. We all did. I touched the one of a kind specially made sterling silver old gnarled vine charm my uncle had made for my aunt last Christmas, the last Christmas they would have shared together. A new bout of tears came rolling out on a loud sob, which triggered more loud sobs from the ladies around me.

When I thought it couldn't get any harder, Sydney handed Jenna a bag. Jenna began pulling little burgundy boxes with silver bows out and the room went still and the air heavy. Sydney pulled out a letter and began reading as Jenna handed each of the ladies a box:

"Raquel updated this letter every year. She was always the planner, always prepared. She really could teach those boy scouts a thing or two."

With tears streaming down her face Sydney began to read:

"My Dearest Tribe,

If you are reading this, it means I am no longer with you. I want each of you to know I love every one of you like my own blood. I cherish each moment I have had with you and thank you all for the support and kindness you all have shown me."

The group let out a collective sob.

"Jenna,

You have been the best friend a gal could ever have asked for. I counted on you and you came through for me more times than I have fingers to count. I never got to return the favor, mostly because you're stubborn and so completely competent that even though we all need you – you don't really need any of us. I know I can call on you to take care of my beloved Antonio and Isabella like they are your own and I leave them in your capable care. Thank you, my loving friend, and I will see you when you come to join me."

Of course, Raquel would never dream her beloved Antonio's life would be taken the same day as hers. The unbelievable tragedy of this day was thick and the sorrow of the day heavy, making it hard to breathe.

How were any of us going to be able to get through this dark day?

"Francesca,"

Oh Lord, a year was a lifetime ago for Francesca: her hubby was now on hospice in their home and wasn't expected to make it much longer. She left him with the hospice nurses only to come to the funeral and was heading straight back. This wasn't going to be good.

"As I'm writing this, we have just learned about Frank's cancer and I hope by the time you're reading this he is completely cured and you two will be off for a second honeymoon"

Looking up from reading with tears wet on her face, Sydney said, "I'm so sorry honey. Do you want me to keep reading?"

"Yes, please I need to hear her last words to me," Francesca cried desperately.

Sydney nodded her head and continued, "I pray for his recovery every night and know you can count on Antonio to help with anything you, Frank and the girls need. Thank you for all of the beautiful holidays and sharing your amazing daughters with me and Antonio. You all are the family we never had. Please watch out for my Antonio – he will be lost without me and will need your loving family to make it through this time. Always know how much I love you and your beautiful family as if you are all my very own. In my heart you are.

Becca,

What can I say my beautiful big-hearted friend? You and I have gone head to head on numerous occasions, but I wouldn't have had it any other way. You have nothing but my love and respect for all the passion and strength you bring to our tribe and all of our rescues. I value the time I've been honored to have with you –

even if some of it was spent arguing. I love you and trust you to protect our sisters. You are in charge of them now. Do me proud sister."

Becca fell into Francesca's arms and the two of them sobbed quietly as Sydney continued.

"Terra,

My beloved oldest friend. You and I have been through it all. You were there the night I first met my Antonio. You stood up with me when I married my beloved Antonio and you were there for each and every argument and fight, he and I had in those early years. You are always there for me, never wavering once. Your love and dedication are a constant strength I can count on and do often. I know you will watch over Antonio. I know that of all of my sisters, how hard this will be for you and I share more years together than even he and I.

Thank you for your unwavering friendship; you made my life happier and I will miss you every day until I see you again.

Stella,

I love you forever. I love you for being a part of our life, always there and ready to lend a hand and pitch in, always the first to show up and help and the last to leave, making sure I wasn't left with any mess. You think I didn't notice, but I noticed every single time. You made my life easier and you did it quietly and lovingly. I know the world has been a harsh place for you, my friend, but I also know you deserve love and laughter and I want you to go out and seek it. Do it for me if not for yourself."

Stella fell apart, doubled over in her grief, so we had a brief break while water and tissues were passed around, Sydney said, "We need to get through this, or we'll be late, and nothing can begin without us there."

Blowing her nose, she gathered herself to the background noise of those who had already heard their part crying softly, and began reading again;

"Juliette,

You and Syd are my two most dependable tribe members. I respect and count on you for so very much. We all do. You carry the burden of being the reasonable one on your shoulders, which can be a heavy load with this group. I know you are going to do some amazing things for our community and our region, and I am devastated beyond belief I am not going to be there to high five you at every one of your amazing achievements. Just remember, my talented friend, to live for yourself as well. You deserve happiness along with your successes. I love you my sweet friend.

Steve and Allistor,

Please know in my heart you two belong to my family. I adopted you both without you knowing years ago and have thanked the Good Lord above every day that He gifted me with the two of you and your friendship. The fellowship you two bring to our tribe is our rock. Without you two, our tribe falls apart. I ask that you watch over my sisters with the love and compassion, and patience, you always have and know: even if it's not said enough, you two are a blessing to this world and we would be a lot better off with more people like you. I love you both dearly. Until I see you again my friends, peace and love.

Sydney,

Last, but certainly not least, you have the burden of carrying out all of my last wishes. I wouldn't trust anyone to do this but you. You have helped me plan and organize and I trust you with every fiber of my being. While you are going through my things and bringing yourself up to speed on the happenings while you've been away, please take it easy on everyone for the things they kept from you, myself included. We only wanted to protect you and minimize the loss you were already feeling while being forced away from your friends and home. We know you would have rushed back for anyone of us and put your own life at risk and we love you too much to do that to you. I know you will see everything out until the end, please try not to fight with Antonio as you carry out…."

"I can't…" Sydney said through her own tears streaming thick down her face.

"Let me help honey." Steve gently took the papers and continued the reading as Allistor wrapped his arms around Sydney and walked her to the couch where the two of them sat down.

"…. please try not to fight with Antonio as you carry out my wishes. Also, please take care of Isabella and give her my charm bracelet before the funeral so she has it to fiddle with – it will give her something of mine to keep close and distract Antonio and might help him not get so angry with everyone who is doing everything wrong. I know I lean on you a lot, and you never complain, but it's only because I trust and respect you and your courage more than any one person on this planet. I love you my sweet friend and I always will. My only regret is the last few years, not seeing your beautiful face if it wasn't on a digital screen. I've missed you more than you will ever know. Thank you for all you are about to do for me, and I am sorry for any grief Antonio gives you – just know, as you care for him and Isabella, you care for me. And I thank you for it.

I don't know what's happened to me, But I do know I've had an amazing life filled with love, friendship and laughter. I wouldn't change one aspect of it. So, as you send me off for the final time, please carry in your hearts the knowledge that I was happy, truly and completely happy and most if it was because of you women sitting in this room. My Women of Wine Country sisters. I love you and I expect you to carry on the tribe and grow it. Do it for me; do it for you, and when you bring in the new sisters make sure you tell them about me, the very first member and founder.

All my love forever and a day,

Raquel Bellini"

"I...I...I was the f-f-f-founder!" Stella cried, then laughed and then cried some more. This was an ongoing tease the two women shared because they actually came up with the idea together during a wine tasting event Stella was setting up at her wine bar, Poured, before my aunt and uncle had ever even met.

"Isabella, the charm bracelet we gave you is your aunt's. I have all of the personal belongings recovered from the crash and it appeared to me everything was horribly damaged except for this, if you can believe it.

However, since your uncle is gone too – I had sterling silver charms made identical to the one your uncle made for your aunt last Christmas with one minor difference – on the base of the trunk of the vine is Raquel and Antonio's initials with a heart. I've had one made for each of us and cuff links made for you, Steve and Allistor. Also, Isabella, I had a new charm bracelet made with this same charm to start your bracelet off. We haven't welcomed any new members to our tribe in a very long time, but we welcome you and hope you will fill your own bracelet with things that represent milestones in your life. They are both yours, to do with as you like." Sydney handed me two burgundy boxes with silver bows. We all opened the boxes and inspected the beautiful charms through tear filled eyes.

Sydney sat next to me and said quietly, "You have your letter Isabella. I wanted you to have it to read privately. Now do you understand why I said to wait?"

I wrapped my arms around her and whispered, "Thank you Sydney."

"Alright ladies. Wipe those snotty noses. We got a sister and her man to bury and a whole lotta fine ass men anxious for us to get the move on," Becca proclaimed in typical Becca fashion: straight forward and to the point.

The funeral was just as elegant as my aunt would have wanted. She'd thought of everything. The church was filled with stunning bouquets of fresh flowers; the service itself was beautiful. People spoke about both my aunt and uncle lovingly and respectfully with a few light-hearted jokes peppered in between the sad stories. I knew my aunt and uncle were pillars of the community, but I didn't realize just how much they did for others. I should've known; I just never really knew how much they contributed.

Shame on me.

A little commotion occurred when Sydney tried slipping the unopened envelope containing the letter Raquel had left for Antonio into his coffin. It was a little bit of a feat with all the flowers piled on top. Roman, Cabe and I held the flowers in place, and the man who was in charge of the casket and keeping everything looking good had a bit of a heart attack, but once he realized what she was up to, ended up helping her by holding the casket lid up while she slipped it in. It was, after all, the right thing to do and there was no way anyone was stopping Sydney from laying that letter to rest with its rightful owner.

I stuck with my aunt's tribe, who sat in the second two rows from the front, leaving the first row on both sides of the church for family. Behind us sat the row of Macho Men who always seemed to be nearby and Antonio's family, from Italy sat in the first row on the isle across from us.

Sydney leaned over and whispered, "Remember the wineries I told you were upset about your uncle selling the fruit to a new buyer? One is sitting over there." She tilted her head indicating a pew across the aisle, three back, "and the other over there," she said, nodding to the aisle directly behind us. I waited a few minutes and stole glances at them both and was shocked to see when I looked at them both sets of people were watching me.

Great.

Just before the service was to begin, Cabe stood, came around to where I was, and held out his hand. I looked to him, his hand, and then back at him before he reached down and lifted my arm from my lap, pulled me up into a standing position, and escorted me to the first pew.

I was a little taken aback by his high handedness, but I didn't want to make a scene, so I sat down and looked at him. I must admit he looked really good in his dark gray suit. It fit him like it was tailored to every plain and muscle on his body. He sat down next to me and draped his arm across the back of my pew space and leaned towards me, like we were an old married couple.

I started to say something when Sydney, followed by Roman, sat down on the other side of me, took my hand in hers and held on. I watched as the rest of the ladies filled up the first pew, so we were once again sitting as a group. Just as Raquel would have wanted.

Well then, I guess this wasn't so bad.

As we listened to the Pastor, and then Raquel and Antonio's friends speak, I was distracted by Cabe, his big strong body sitting next to mine, and the subtle manly-spice scent he had coming off of him. This was not the worst distraction I'd ever had.

From the church we all went to the graveside where once again, Cabe took charge by guiding me to the front row and the middle seat. I ended up sitting wedged between him and Sydney. And when that ceremony was over, I was guided back to the car by Cabe with a hand at my lower back, into the car he wanted me in (with him) and then back to Bellini Estates for the reception.

He never, not once, left my side, which did freak me out a little, but was also not horrible. He seemed to have a never-ending stash of fresh tissue. And he also seemed to know when I needed someone to stop crying all over me and move on, and he made that happen.

Sometimes, depending on the person and level of emotion, not very politely, but still, it was kind of nice.

Before long I watched in a daze as the cars began pulling away as everyone left to go to the reception. It was just us gals and Macho Men left at the grave site for our final goodbyes to Raquel and Antonio.

We became aware that Francesca was having a harder time than we realized. She was overwhelmed at the grave site, and anxious to get back to her husband. One by one we hugged her and tried to console her. But honestly, how do you console a woman who has to leave the grave site of one of her best friends, to rush home to her husband who laid dying in hospice care?

"Lucas, can you get Francesca home?" I heard Cabe say quietly. "I don't want her driving." This prompted a low discussion between the Macho Men. Dark shades covered all of their somber faces and their large bodies were clad in varying styles of dark suits.

"I'll take her." Lucas, I noted, wore a black suit with a black shirt and a black patterned tie, combined with his dark shades and black hair he looked intensely sinister.

I slipped my hand onto Cabe's shoulder and asked, "Will she be okay with him?"

For the first time since I arrived, I saw Cabe's smile. A big white brilliant smile. And as soon as it came it left. Just like that.

"You don't have to worry about Lucas or any of my guys. Well, except maybe Marcus, he hangs with dogs all day. How sane can he be?"

"Saner than you." Came a grumble from next to me. Now I knew which one Marcus was.

"Thank you." I said to Cabe. I was learning this is what he did; quietly took care of everyone.

And it was so sweet.

"Maybe I should go with her?" Jenna said.

Cabe's dark lenses landed on Jenna, "Have Lucas give you his number. He'll come back and pick you up when you're ready to leave."

Sweet again!

I was so thankful for all of them. The Macho Men and Sydney and the Women of Wine Country tribe. They had executed everything so beautifully, so brilliantly, exactly as Raquel would have wanted.

But danggit! As nice as they were; Macho Men were also seriously *Bossy* with a capital B!

CHAPTER 4

In or Out

After the reception, the Women of Wine Country tribe and both of Antonio's sisters in law stayed to help finish cleaning up. They worked quickly to set the kitchens straight after the catering company left. With the group of this size, it didn't take long. Once the work was done, the sisters in law hugged us all and then escaped to their rooms to be with their husbands.

I didn't realize it, but some of the men had stayed as well and were in the courtyard smoking cigars and drinking whisky – this was something they did often with Antonio and it was their own private "send-off" to a man they all respected and would be terribly missed.

Slowly, one by one, the wine tribe and Macho Men left. It was well after midnight and after the events of the last two days, I was so tired I could barely keep my eyes focused. Sydney was arguing with her really handsome big guy, Roman. and it looked like he was getting ready to drag her off into one of the vineyards.

I made myself a cup of tea and took it to an empty table in the courtyard. I was just settling in when I felt big hands on my shoulders and a kiss planted on the top of my head. "You know you can go to bed. We can lock up - Syd and I are both staying here tonight."

Beautiful Cabe Brown sat down at my table, reached down grabbed my crossed ankles and pulled my feet into his lap. I was so shocked by this whole touchy-feely version of Cabe he'd been laying on me all day. I wasn't sure what to do next, so I did what I'd been doing all day with him and sat still as he pulled my shoes off and began rubbing my tired feet.

Cabe and his band of Macho Men had been shuffling us gals around all day, staying on the outskirts of our emotional group but never too far away. They always had the cars ready; they took care of getting Francesca home and Jenna back to the estate and took care of any other need we might have. I never once had to ask for a tissue, or water, or cup of tea; Cabe or one of his team of Macho Men were always there thrusting whatever we needed into our hands before we could ask.

Against my will, I let out a great big giant moan and sank deeper into my chair.

"Oh My God." I moaned again as he hit the sorest part of my poor foot. Surprised by my outburst, I looked at him and saw that he was looking down examining his large dark hands on my pale feet.

It was a fascinating contrast. His hands were way bigger than my feet and I wasn't a small girl – I wore a size nine and a half, but his hands were so large they completely engulfed my feet.

"You're staying here too?" I asked, as he continued rubbing at the soreness.

"Both Syd and I are."

"I knew Sydney was staying, but I didn't know you were, why are you staying?"

"I like to make sure Syd is safe." I waited for him to expand, but since I knew some of what had happened to her, I didn't ask, and he didn't offer.

"Did you stay here last-night too?" I asked, curious.

"I was here. As long as Syd is here, I will be here."

"Oh. Okay." What else was there to say?

"Your mother is going to show up at some point you know," he surprised me by saying.

I dropped my feet from his lap and sat up reaching down to slip my shoes back on.

"You know about my momma?"

"I do."

"Well, my momma is my problem and I will deal with her when she shows up."

"Deal with her like you have your whole life?"

"What does that mean?"

"You've allowed your relationship with your mother to hold you back from advancing anything in your life. Is that what Raquel and Antonio would want you to do now?"

What. The. Fuck!

"You don't know what I've allowed my momma to do or not do," I said, standing up. He was right, but it was pretty much bullshit that he was calling me out on it ...especially now, after just burying my beautiful aunt.

"I know every single thing your mother has kept you from doing. I know every boyfriend she stopped you from getting serious about; I know about every apartment she got you kicked out of; I know about every job you've left because of her and I know you finished your degree secretly just so she wouldn't ruin it for you." He'd grabbed my wrist and kept me from stomping off while he was saying this. I was standing and he was still sitting, so I leaned over him pointed my finger in his face and said, "You don't know ANYTHING about me." I was shaking and emotional and just didn't need his shit, on top of all the other shit that had been my life up until this point.

Still hanging onto my wrist, he stood and pulled me forward until I bumped into his chest and he wrapped an arm around my waist, holding me firm against him.

"What are you..."

"Hush," He said in his deep gravelly voice, giving me a little squeeze. "I wasn't insulting you. I know all about you. I met you when you were a teenager and have listened to both Raquel and Antonio fret and worry over you for years. I listened to them justify to themselves how you stopped coming to visit because it would cause problems for you with your mother, without once considering what they were going through. You always put her first, to your detriment, and that of everyone around you. Now you've inherited this big place. With all this money, don't you think for a second that mother of yours isn't going to show up here to get every last dime she can. Along the way, humiliating and defiling you like she's done your whole life for sport. You aren't as smart as your aunt and uncle thought you were, if you think any different. And if that's the case sell Bellini Estate to someone who cares about it and just go away." He suddenly released me thrusting me away from him. Stared at me a second with his intense grey eyes, turned and walked off.

I teetered a bit on my heels and sat back down. Shocked.

Stunned.

How dare he! Who did he think he was to speak to me this way and lay this on me the same day we'd buried my only sane family members?

He pissed me right the heck off .... but I knew why I was so upset... I was pissed because he was RIGHT.

I had done exactly that!

Exactly.

Sometimes, I guess it takes a stranger to show you who you really are – what you look like.

And it wasn't pretty. It was ugly. I was ugly.

It was a sobering moment for me. I was suddenly wide awake and everything was crystal clear.

Everything.

My momma.

My aunt and her friends.

My aunt and her love for my uncle, this beautiful place and life they had built.

The fact that Cabe was right.

My momma *was* gonna come here and work as hard as she could to destroy it all; she would do it just for sport. For the enjoyment of tearing down everything my beautiful, hardworking, loving aunt had built.

Well fuck that.

The *least* I was gonna do was keep her from destroying everything my aunt had worked so hard for. The *most* I was gonna do was build on their legacy and do everything in my power to model myself after my aunt and make sure her memory stayed alive. I vowed it right then, the very same night I buried Raquel and Antonio. I vowed it to the heavens; I knew they were both looking down and watching me. I vowed I would not let my aunt, who believed in me more than I believed in me, down. I made a solemn vow to be the woman Raquel always told me I could be and believed I was. I vowed it to her memory, my uncle's memory and to the land I was standing on and would now call home.

I was NOT going to let them down! Not one more time.

I didn't exactly know how I was gonna pull it off, but I knew I had the tribe and Sydney to help me. I also had Antonio's brothers and they wanted this winery to continue on, just as I did. They were proud of what their brother had built, and I knew they would help me too.

I got myself and my aching feet to my room, jumped in the shower to wash the day of grief from my body, clear my mind and prepare for the next day, which was going to be the first day of the rest of my life.

The new me.

A strong capable version of me.

I was going to become the woman Raquel had always thought I was. I knew I wasn't her yet, but I could fake being her until I was her.

Dressing in shorts and camisole sleep set, I fell asleep as soon as my head hit the fluffy pillow.

I awoke suddenly when I heard a loud banging and sirens. I realized quickly the banging was someone at my bedroom door and the sirens were some type of alarm. I jumped out of bed and flung the door wide open to find one of Antonio's brothers yelling at me in Italian, which I did not understand. He was yelling and gesturing, and then he took off running down the hall, so I ran after him, down the stairs, and out the front door. What hit me first was the strong smell of smoke.

Then I saw the blaze in the vineyard.

"NO!" I screamed and ran as fast as I could in my bare feet towards flames so high, they were lightening up the dark sky.

A fire!

A fire was burning my uncle's prized old vines.

His treasured vines, the ones he coveted. The vines he loved so much he only handpicked, and hand pruned, the same vines that ...... *Jumpin' Jezebels!*

The grapes!

Antonio's precious grapes were on fire! How could this be happening?

I ran as fast as I could towards the crowd of men working at the fire, the flames licked violently towards the night sky, consuming my uncles' precious old vines. The heat coming off of the fire was unbearable and took all my will not to run from it. The smoke stung my eyes and made it hard to breathe.

How in the heck do old as dirt vines suddenly catch on fire? This couldn't be happening! Breathing hard, my palms were itching to do something...*anything.*

Standing there watching the vines burning and all the activity around me; I was frozen. I couldn't move, but in my head, I was screaming DO SOMETHING!

I just didn't know *what* I could do. "Okay Isabella," I whispered to myself, "Get it together and look for what needs to be done."

I could see they had hoses coming from all different areas and the watering drip lines had been turned on. But the water was barely making a difference – the fire was continuing to grow. I watched as a flame jumped to a new vine and the leaves immediately began to brown and curl.

I was close to the fire and the heat was so great, I thought for sure the hair on my arms, legs and face were going to be singed off.

Suddenly, a large tanker truck skidded to a stop right behind me throwing dirt everywhere and bringing me out of my trance. I watched as a shirtless, shoe-less Cabe jumped from the truck, unwound a huge hose, attached it to the tank, and yelled "All Clear" as he unleashed a wide stream of water hitting the fire and causing a giant mushroom of steam and smoke to choke out everyone present and drive us back a few feet away from the area.

I watched frantically, my eyes tracking everything at once, my mind toggling back and forth between praying to God for the safety of the vines and screaming silently in frustrated panic.

It didn't take long before the water from the truck and the other hoses had the fire under control. And as the last cinders were doused the fire engines arrived with lights and sirens. Well, I guess that explains why my uncle would need his own water truck. Thank God Cabe had spent the night!

The firemen who arrived went straight to Cabe. He was busy making sure everyone who was pitching in to fight the fire was okay and no one had been hurt. I took note that he went out of his way to check on everyone, shaking their hand or slapping them hard on the back, in that way men do that seems like it hurts, but was a sign of affection.

As I approached the man huddle, I overheard Cabe saying, "...and I could smell the accelerant when I arrived. It was set purposely. The grapes haven't been picked yet, but the fruit has been sold, so I need to confirm what was used to minimize further damage to the vineyard."

"You got it Cabe, Stanford and Cunningham will check to make sure the fire is completely out and there aren't any chances of re-ignition. We will work as quickly as possible and try to keep from hurting any more vines. This is a real shame. Especially now...." The Fire Captain's eyes dropped to me and he stopped talking.

Cabe followed the captain's eyes to me and squinted.

"Ma'am, I'm Captain Hernandez." He reached out his hand to shake mine.

"I'm Isabella. This is my aunt and uncle's vineyard." I said as his large hand engulfed mine in a gentle but firm handshake.

"I am very sorry for your loss ma'am. They both were very highly thought of and were big supporters of the fire district."

I hiccupped a small sob and said, "Thank you very much."

The Fire Captain turned back to Cabe and said, "I'll let you know when we complete the investigation."

"You'll let me know." I said and they both turned to me.

"Excuse me ma'am?"

"I am now the owner of Bellini Estates and want to be the one notified as soon as you know anything about this fire," I replied in as strong and firm voice as I could.

I watched Cabe from the corner of my eye as he crossed his arms over his chest and turned his full attention to me. The sun was just making break and the sky had become lighter, making it easier to see, than just moments before. His eyes landed on my chest and he suddenly dropped his arms and stepped forward and in front of me and barked "Isabella go back to the house and get dressed."

Cabe's reaction made me look down at my chest. Jumpin' Jezebels!

My camisole had gotten wet and was clinging to my chest and you could see right through it. Crossing my arms over my breasts, I was ready to say something smart-ass back to Cabe when the sweet, and I might add handsome, Captain Hernandez placed a large jacket over my shoulders, and pulled it closed over my arms at my chest.

"Here you go ma'am." He said.

"Thank you, that was very kind of you." I said softly to him and then glared at Cabe, who was now scowling at the Fire Captain.

The Fire Captain looked to Cabe, back to me and then smiled a big handsome guy smile and said, "Anytime ma'am. I'll be happy to call you when I have some information about the fire. Do you have a number

I can reach you?" I gave him my number, all the while ignoring Cabe, who had turned his scowl to both the Fire Captain and myself.

"As soon as the sun is fully up, I will have Rafael and his guys here to take stock on how much we lost and we will need to get with Sydney about the contract sale and see what this means for the winery," Cabe said through clenched teeth and turned to go.

I placed my hand on his bare arm to turn him back and said, "Thank you Cabe. Thank you for all of this. I honestly don't know what we would have done without you"

Cabe watched me for a moment and then on a deep sigh, draped his arm over my shoulders, tucked me in under his arm and walked me back to the house with his arm around my shoulders.

Macho Men were handy to have around, but sure were fickle.

CHAPTER 5

Home

The next morning was a busy frantic experience. The reading of the will was scheduled for five pm. The whole estate was active and bustling, getting set up for harvest and dealing with the events that had already been scheduled. I never went back to sleep after the fire. Instead, I dressed in comfortable clothing; matching salmon colored yoga pants and a tank top, made tea, and went to Antonio's large old fashioned, heavy wood lined office where the beautiful diffused morning sun streamed in through the old warped seeded glass windows. I sat in his giant Merlot colored high back leather chair and began writing at his huge antique dark wood desk. I made lists of what I knew I had to take care of, lists of the questions I needed to ask, and lists of the people I thought could and would, help me in designated areas.

By the time Sydney found me, I was finishing up my game plan, and had it pretty well organized and was ready to start moving forward.

"Good morning Bella," Sydney said from the doorway with a hot cup of coffee cradled in her hands, a loudly purring Agatha weaving her way through Sydney's ankles. "I understand we had a fire last night?" That was Sydney, always cool as a cucumber – nothing riled her. Good, I was going to need her cool composure to help me.

Come to think of it – I didn't remember seeing her at the fire.

Wow, I handled all that myself. "Yes, where were you?" I asked.

She waved the question away with a flick of her wrist and instead of answering asked me, "What are you working on?"

Interesting.

"Well, the way I see it, I have until five today before everyone in the world officially knows I now own and operate Bellini Estates." She nodded her agreement. "So, I am going to work every minute until then, getting things in place so when everyone comes at me for whatever thing they think they can get from me. Basically, I'm shoring up my defenses."

Slanting her head to the side, she looked hard at me, "Smart girl."

"Come in and let me show you what I have now, and you can tell me what you think I've missed. The fire last night was set on purpose in the old vines. If it weren't for Cabe, we would have lost so much more than we did."

"Good Ol' Cabe always riding in on his white horse to save the day."

"Everything okay with you two?" I asked, tilting my head.

"Yes, I shouldn't have said that. Cabe is a great guy who saved my life. Just be careful, sometimes the decisions he makes on your behalf, in order to keep you safe, aren't necessarily the decisions we would make for ourselves." She entered the office and sat in the chair facing me, opposite the desk.

"Duly noted," I said, not exactly sure what the heck we were talking about but wanting to move on to my issues since I was on a limited time frame. I could come back to this and made a mental note to do just that.

"So, listen, I have already spoken to Antonio's brothers, who, by the way, have informed me through their wives they are my uncles too - my tias and tios," I smiled a sad grateful smile at Sydney, who smiled the same sad grateful smile back, "and asked them to help get me through this harvest. Francisco and Sophia are staying to do just that and Santini and Gloria are heading back to Italy to take care of their winery. So that's going to help immensely." I smiled, "Turns out I have a whole lot more family than I ever realized." It was fantastic I had them and disappointing how much I had let myself miss out on.

"Moving on...I need to be introduced to the harvesters, wine making crew, bottling group and walked through the process. I did some research this morning and found sommelier classes only forty minutes away from here I can attend to help me learn about wines. Unfortunately, they're already full this year. However, I contacted them to see if they had any Master Sommeliers in the area and turns out they do, I mean how weird is that? Master wine sommeliers in wine country, who would have figured?" I smiled at Sydney who was watching me pretty closely, but not responding to my little joke. "Anyway... they are sending me a list of the ones located within a thirty-minute radius. I'm gonna see if I can hire one of them to come and teach me about wines in order to get me through until I can get signed up with some classes."

"Smart. Might I also suggest you contact Stella? She is a Sommelier as well." Sydney took a sip of her coffee and crossed her legs without saying anything else, so I responded, "Wow that's perfect! I'll get a hold of her tomorrow and see what kind of time she has available."

"Also, who would be my go-to person around here? Like the person who knows the staff and can tell me who works where?" I asked.

"Raquel's assistant Stacy – I'll see if she is here today. She might be in the kitchen. I instructed the staff to continue performing their normal duties until they were told differently."

"Okay, first I'll need a breakdown of the different employees and what departments they work in. Then I need to have duties and see where we need to hire or pick up from where Raquel and Antonio left off."

"I can help gather the employees. Might I suggest you have everyone who is on staff meet together at once and go from there?"

"I'd prefer to meet them all in smaller groups and meet by departments. It will make it easier for me to differentiate who belongs in Antonio's part of the estate and who worked for Raquel, which employees are household staff etc.," I replied looking down at my list. "I've made a list of what I believe are the departments. Once I get a chance to identify the main players for each department, I can expand the lists I have – it'll help me stay organized."

"Isabella, look at me."

I looked up from my many lists.

"You flew in the day before yesterday, buried Raquel and Antonio yesterday, dealt with a fire last night and this morning you have completely recharged yourself and are taking the bull by the horns without missing a beat."

I nodded at her.

Little did she know I was doing this for my aunt, making up for all I hadn't done. I knew it was too late to go back and fix things, but that wasn't going to stop me from making Raquel's name and hard work shine on. "Have you read Raquel's letter yet?" she asked.

I shook my head and said, "I can't. I need to be strong right now and it will crumble me. And also…. I need to prove I deserve to receive a letter from her, before I reward myself with reading it."

She watched me for a moment before saying, "I'm very proud of you."

It took me back a minute, first, because I didn't deserve anyone to be proud of me, and second, because I hadn't really done anything yet. I said, "No one except my aunt has ever uttered those words to me; I'll try to live up them."

Sydney rose from her chair, placed her coffee on my uncle's desk, came around and hugged me so tight I couldn't breathe. She whispered at the top of my head, "I will never forget to tell you how proud I am of you."

Letting me go, she picked up her coffee and walked out with Agatha trailing behind her.

After a brief meeting with Rafael and the farm employees, I learned that only a small number of the vines were damaged and even smaller number lost, thanks to the quick action of everyone at the fire. They were very busy taking sugar content samplings of the grapes in the adjacent area of the fire, because I was told the heat from the fire would alter the grapes of the nearby vines. The vines weren't lost, but some of the grapes might be.

I then met with Francisco and Sophia, who were working on getting the crush area staged and tanks set up. I found Cabe in the middle of the staging area taking count of the blue picking bins and the large white receiving bins.

"Hey, what are you doing?" I said as I approached him.

He looked up from his clipboard and said, "Just lending a hand, so when it's time for the grapes to be harvested, we're ready, Antonio usually did this, and I would often come out and help during the harvest."

"I didn't know that. Thank you."

"You didn't know because you weren't around. Antonio and I were great friends. He was an honorable man and I won't have his legacy destroyed." He gave me a hard look, flipped his pages over the clip board and walked away.

Well shit. Someone was grumpy.

I wasn't sure what I did to deserve that, but I had too much to do and needed to stay focused.

Next was the catering staff meeting. Stacy was a Godsend in this area; she'd compiled a list for me of all of the upcoming events, their menus, projected cost vs income, and the staff assigned to each event along with their job duties. She also had instructed the staff to wear name tags so I could familiarize myself with them. It seemed the staff in the catering business could take over for the most part on everything except for my aunt's duties. Stacy approached me and said, "Raquel had two interviews this week for bakery chefs. Up until now she had been doing the baking, but she was getting too busy to keep it up. What do you want me to do about the appointments?"

"Let's keep them. If you can sit in on the interviews with me, we can decide together who will work out best. In the short term, I can actually chip in as far as baking and cooking." It's something the three of us, my aunt, my momma and myself, all know how to do really well, and my fondest memories were of us in the kitchen. I continued, "I'm not saying I'll be anywhere as good as my Aunt, and I'm not sure if I'm good enough to do it full time, but I can pitch in for the short term."

I started to go and turned back to Stacy. "Thank you so much for your efficiency, and all you're doing to help." I gave her a brief hug and started to walk away, but turned back again and said, "Also, can you please ask the rest of the winery staff to wear name tags too? It was a brilliant idea!"

Her smile was the answer I needed, so I went on to the rest of my day. It was pretty much the same as the first part, meetings with staff trying to figure out what was going on and where I was needed most.

Luckily, Stacy immediately had everyone wearing badges, color coded by department; it was already making things much more comfortable.

After a long day, I showered, applied light makeup, dressed in a simple flowing black, tank maxi dress, and slipped a pair of low-heeled strappy sandals. I pulled my hair back into a high ponytail, slid some pearl studs into my ears, and headed down to my uncle's library where the reading of the will was taking place.

The room was completely filled. I hadn't realized so many people would be here and were in the will. Maybe Sydney was wrong, maybe the estate was going to be willed out to everyone?

The library was standing room only, so I slipped into the room and leaned up against the back wall.

Soon Sydney got started. "Good evening. You have all been asked here because each one of you have been named in the will of either Antonio Bellini, Raquel Bellini or both. I will read the will and the items you are inheriting, and I ask that you leave the room directly after. If you have any questions, please feel free to email those questions to my email address listed on my card – I will not be answering any questions verbally. Any and all questions will need to be in writing, and in turn, my responses will be in writing," She looked around the room and said, "I can't stress this enough."

Taking a deep breath, she started calling individuals in the room and listed their inheritance.

For the most part, it was some cash to charities that had been favorites – a few of the rental homes my aunt and uncle owned were left to long time employees, and finally, the children of some of the employees were set up with college funds to make sure the immigrants' children would be able to receive a higher education. This was most of the crowd. When the list of college funds was read off, the mothers of the recipients wailed long and loud. I teared up – it was hard not too – Raquel and Antonio were extremely generous and thought of everyone. They loved and cared for all of their employees as if they were family. One by one, the room cleared out until eventually all that was left was me, Cabe and Sydney.

I walked further into the room and sat down. Cabe stayed standing against the wall across the room. "Cabe, Bella, this may come to a surprise to you both, but Raquel and Antonio left the winery to you, both of you."

"WHAT!" Cabe yelled as he pushed off the wall.

I sat there quietly, not really sure what was going on.

"Antonio wanted to make sure you, Cabe, had a vested interest in the winery, so you would stay around and make sure it was run properly. Raquel knew it was part of his wishes and they agreed. Of course, they thought you'd be helping Raquel, not Bella, but regardless, the terms stand. Now your portion is a non-voting stock ownership, so basically Bella owns most of the winery but this way they thought it would be fair and would limit how much you would be able to bulldoze Raquel," she gestured toward me, "now our Bella."

She turned to me, "Quite frankly most of these provisions, regarding you Isabella, were set up as if Raquel passed first. They both knew you wouldn't have anyone to turn to. If you had been married, they left a provision for that but since you're still single, they don't apply. They wanted to make sure whoever inherited had help. They knew Cabe loved this place and they knew he knew the winery like the back of his hand, and they wanted to have his protection. So, they left him twenty five percent of the winery and you seventy five percent." She stopped speaking and watched us both for a moment before saying,

"Anyway, you two have to figure out how to work together and navigate. They also left a provision for Cabe to move to the estate..."

"WHAT THE HELL?" Now it was my turn to yell.

"Yes, seems they wanted to make sure he was close by. If you don't move in and live the first year here at the winery in the house, then you forfeit the inheritance."

"Me too?" I asked

"No, just him." Sydney pointed a perfectly manicured finger at Cabe who was still as a statue. "Bella, Raquel and Antonio were worried about your mother and her influence over you. This provision with Cabe was just to protect you."

"Wait a minute. I have men deployed all over the world. It's impossible to expect me to leave my business and responsibilities and move in here to playhouse with Isabella."

"Cabe, you can set up command central here and run SDI from the estate. You need to look at this as the last thing you're ever going to be able to do for Antonio. He counted on you." Sydney said.

I understood where they were coming from, I hadn't ever shown them any kind of back bone and always gave into my momma and her crazy ass ways – even when it was bad for me. Of course, they would be worried. Of course, they would put a strong man with me who knew the estate as well as Cabe did.

And even though it seemed outdated and old fashioned, and a bit chauvinistic, I understood.

"I understand," I turned to Cabe, "please stay, stay and help and I promise I won't let you or them down."

Cabe turned his big man body towards me and said, "Isabella, I can stay and help, but you need to understand that I also have a business. I'll help – but this isn't going to become my life. I will do it for my friendship with Antonio and Raquel but if I see one hint of you wavering or making bad decisions you won't like what I do next."

"I understand." And I did. I needed to prove where my heart was, and I needed to prove that I would stand up to my momma when she decided to show up – and she would. She always did.

These words it seemed, had magical powers and conjured my momma because the next thing we heard was;

"Where is my baby? I know she's here! Let me in you stupid! *Asshole! Bitch!* you've no right to keep me out! This is my family home and I'll be let in! You are FIRED BITCH - FIRED!!"

Jumpin' Jezebels!

There she was.

The three of us went still for a second and then in unison we all headed for the door.

CHAPTER 6

Vintage Vines

There she was, my momma, in all her glory, yelling and cussing and spitting her fury at poor Stacy, the unfortunate soul who had stayed late to help with the people receiving an inheritance, and happened to answer the door.

My beautiful and clearly drunk momma, and her beau Mark standing behind her. She must have consumed a gallon of alcohol on the plane; I could smell it from where I was standing behind Stacy.

Cabe gently pulled Stacy away from the door and told her to get her things and go on home. As she walked by me, I pulled her in for a hug and apologized – something I did by rote – I was so used to apologizing to people for my momma's bad behavior.

Sydney started first, "Cynthia, I told you not to come. You were not included in the will and inherited nothing from your sister or her husband."

"The hell you say! This is MY sister's home and MY daughter. I will come in. I will stay in my family home and I WILL be contesting that fucking will. So, don't be handing anything out yet, cause you're gonna look real fucking dumb when you gotta go ask for it all back." She said this in a spitting nasty way, wobbling her head back and forth in an effort to punctuate her statement.

God. I was so sick of this.

"Shut up." I said.

"What-the-fuck did *you* just say to *me* girl?" She spat.

"I said shut up. Shut up. Shut up. SHUT UP! You are NOT welcome here. You WILL leave and not come back." I stepped closer to her pointing my finger in her chest and said, "If you don't leave now, I'll call the police, have you removed and then I'll have a stay-away order issued against you." I was done with her bullshit. She cost me my valuable time with Raquel. She wasn't costing me anything else.

Sydney stepped back between us when my momma screamed back at me, "Don't you dare fucking talk to me like that you uppity little bitch. You been here only a few days and you think you're all that? Well, let me tell you - you ain't shit, bitch. And when I get this winery, I'm going to kick you and your fancy ass out on the street and let you see what it's like to fend for yourself.

I've been taking care of you your whole damned life. You ain't ever had to do anythin' for yourself you - little fucking bitch."

I pushed in front of Sydney and got really close to my momma. I could smell the alcohol reeking off of her and saw she was swaying. She was smashed in the worst way. I wasn't even sure she was going to remember any of this. Mark stepped up behind her and held on to her upper arms, probably realizing, the same as me, that any minute she was going to fall over.

"Isabella," Mark said quietly, "Let us in, sweetheart. This is no way to treat your momma."

Looking him in the eye over my momma's head, I said, "I'm sorry she talked you into coming all this way Mark. She was told not to come, and she isn't welcome. You need to get her a room and sober her up. I will talk to her when she isn't stinkin' drunk."

He started to say something else to me when Cabe stepped in front of me and pulled me behind him. "What are you doing here?" He said in a dark manner, a manner in which I had not heard him speak before, and let's just say for future reference, never wanted to hear again.

"Oh, this is just perfect. I should have known the great White Knight Cabe Brown would be here to rescue the beautiful, newly wealthy, damsel in distress. How convenient." This was from Mark and said in a way I had not heard from him either! And it was NOT nice!

What was happening?

The two males stood straight and tall, with their chests puffed out and shoulders back – Mark still had a hold of momma, but seemed to not realize she was starting to slump – her drunken state was going south quickly.

Momma, not caring one bit that there was a badass standoff happening, and she was smack dab in the middle of it, was only able to focus on the fact that if she didn't get another drink in her soon, she was going to pass out - started up again, "Look here, I needa comin an sit 'fore I fall."

"No," Cabe stated, "You two leave now and don't come back." Then he slammed the door right in their faces.

I heard some muffled yelling, but it seemed to move away from the door pretty quickly.

Cabe turn to me, put his large hand flat against my chest and pushed me backwards into the living room right off the entry. "Hey," I started and went to move away when he took both my upper arms and gently shook me. "Hush."

Jumping Jezebels! What was he pissed about now?

"You hush!" I yelled at him, trying unsuccessfully to knock his hands off of me. "I just had my drunken momma show up cussing at me and it seems you know her boyfriend. How is it possible you know her boyfriend from TEXAS?" I finished, still yelling.

"Yes Cabe, I'd like to know the answer to that as well," Sydney said from behind us. She had been quietly watching all of the going's on.

"You know Mark, Syd, you just don't remember – he's Stan Markin's cousin, the one who goes after the vines and wineries when the Markins decide they want to buy up. You went up against him seven years ago, the first time they came after Antonio's Old Vineyards."

"Oh my God. THAT was Mark Sephos?" She asked and tilted her head like she does when she is thinking about something important. I'd picked up on a couple of her cues the past week.

"Why would someone who lives here, knows this area and winery, be in Texas and become a boyfriend of my mommas?" I asked.

"Why indeed?" Sydney responded.

"This is not fucking good at all." Cabe said finally releasing my arms. "Let's sit down and talk this out. This just got a lot more complicated."

"I'll put some coffee and water for tea on," Sydney said, walking away towards the kitchen.

I followed Cabe into the living room as Sydney took off to the kitchen.

"I want you to stop grabbin' a hold of me," I said as I sat down on the sofa. My southern accent coming on stronger because I was upset.

Cabe watched me as I sat so I watched him right back.

"I don't grab you," He replied clearly offended that I was offended.

"Yes, you do. You grab a hold o' me, guide me, pull me, and for the most part find any reason to put your hands on me whenever we are together – now you may remember me from my visits when I was young, but I don't remember you, and where I come from its rude to put your hands on people without their permission."

I waited for a response, but when none came, I continued on, "We are gonna to be working together. I want to make sure Raquel and Antonio's memories are kept alive. I know you don't think much of me, have doubts about me and my abilities, and I really do understand why you would have those doubts. I'll have to show you and Sydney what I'm capable of, but in the meantime, you've got to stop grabbin' me. Okay?" I was trying to appeal to his sensitive nature, hoping he had one. I hadn't really seen one yet, but he was Antonio's good friend and hopefully he would come around sooner rather than later.

Leaning towards me, and after what seemed like an eternity of him staring at me in uncomfortable silence, Cabe asked quietly in his deep voice, "Why don't you like my hands on you, Isabella?"

"Well, I..." My traitorous body flushed, making me even more uncomfortable. Shit, what was happening here? Was I misreading something?

"Coffee's on and here is a nice hot cup of tea for you, Bella. What'd I miss?" she asked, looking from Cabe to me and back again.

Cabe leaned back and said, "Seems Isabella doesn't like me touching her."

Raising her eyebrows at me Sydney said, "Well, that's got to be a new experience for you Cabe, finally meeting a woman who doesn't want you touching her."

"Whatever." I mumbled, relaxing back with my tea into the comfortable couch.

Sydney sat next to me and said, "Me thinks nefarious acts are afoot."

"Tell me how y'all know Mark." I said.

"Mark is related to and part of the Markin Winery and Estate. They have been trying to buy up your uncle's old vines for years. They are the ones Antonio used to sell the fruit from the old vines. Old Man Markin and Antonio had a great relationship, but when his son Stan took over, Stan and Antonio butted heads, causing Antonio to switch to selling the old vine fruit to Vista Rio Ranch. That turned out to be a good fit and they'd purchased the fruit for the last couple of years. Antonio had seventy-five acres DNA tested at Syd's insistence, and learned that they were indeed Cinsault Vines. They may well be the oldest Cinsault Vines in the world. This of course brought their value up dramatically, and turned the filler fruit into a highly sought-after vintage vine, increasing the price significantly." When Cabe finished, he looked at me.

"Are all the grapes...er... fruit already contracted out with the new buyers?" I asked.

"No, your uncle held back ten acres for himself," Sydney replied. "He wanted to experiment with the wine and see how it would differ in taste between the French oak and American oak barrels."

"How many tons was he averaging per acre from these vines?" I asked thinking about the research I had completed that afternoon.

"Those vines produced an average of four tons per acre," Sydney replied, looking at me intensely with her head cocked sideways. Even though the look freaked me out a little bit, I was starting to get used to her watching me this way.

"That's pretty good for old vines isn't it?" I asked.

"Yes. Typically, six tons per acre is what we look for, so to have one hundred and fifty-year-old vines; still putting out four tons an acre is a testament to Antonio and Rafael's genius in the vineyard and their devotion to quality over quantity," Cabe said, getting up and heading to the kitchen for coffee.

Wow. He really did know a lot about the vineyards.

"Okay. Let's go back to how Mark knows you all and how it's possible he is now my momma's boyfriend?"

"My guess is the prick hooked up with your mother in order to gain access to the vineyard. What I can't figure out is how he was going to do that. Everyone knew your aunt and her sister didn't get along. How long ago did your mom and Mark start dating?" Cabe asked, as he walked back into the room and handed a steaming cup to Sydney.

"I think it's been about two months. They were nice and settled in and cozy like, but still in the 'momma hiding her crazy' portion of the relationship, so it couldn't have been any longer than that," I said, sipping my tea.

"This just doesn't make sense. Why would the Markin family go after Isabella and her mother, when everyone knows they haven't even been here for a visit in years?" Sydney asked.

"That's a very good question. I'm getting the feeling I'd better have the car your aunt and uncle were driving looked at and maybe the bodies examined," Cabe said.

"What?" I breathed, comprehending what that statement implied.

"Okay, let's just get through the rest of the night without totally freaking Isabella out. She's been through quite enough," Sydney said, as she sat next to me and wrapped her arms around my shoulders.

I laid my head against hers and asked, "When're the hits gonna quit comin'?"

"I don't have the answer to that, my beautiful Bella. I'm sorry, I wish I did," she whispered to me.

"Cabe," I asked, "do you think my aunt and uncle were killed?"

"I sure fucking hope not. If someone ended them on purpose, that someone is going to pay big - fucking - time."

"Cabe?" I asked.

When he looked at me, I said, "You say fuck a lot."

CHAPTER 7

She Can Cook

After the upsetting discussion the evening my momma showed up and reared her drunken head, things seemed to get into a rhythm.

First, we had events scheduled every evening, with the tasting room open to the public Thursday thru Sunday.

This kept me busy, learning the business and getting myself familiarized with Raquel's kitchens. Both kitchens were top of the line and almost identical: white cabinetry with stainless steel pulls, on stainless steel counter-tops, top of the line appliances; a stove top with eight industrial burners, four huge convection ovens and an indoor rotisserie. There was a walk-in freezer/cooler, and the gleaming floors were finished in a high gloss deep red wine concrete. Shiny pots and pans hung from racks over the large island. Herbs grew in the vast bay window above the sink. French doors led to a spacious patio, with a table and chairs, overlooking the large full vegetable and herb garden, that was lined with fruit trees.

The kitchens were magnificent, and this was the best time so far; I felt the closest to my aunt in her kitchens. It was like I was back baking with her. Every now and again I thought I'd catch a faint whiff of her perfume. I told myself she was there watching over me, so I started talking to her while I was looking through the cabinets for ingredients. It was nice and took me to a place where I could forget for a just a moment all that had happened, all that had been lost, all that I'd lost. If anyone thought it was weird, they kept it to themselves.

I made extra pastry brie and raspberry bites, prime rib single skewers with blue cheese, crab stuffed mushrooms and tiny one bite pecan pies for the tasting room. I took extra care and time and arranged it all on my aunt's beautiful pewter multi-tiered serving platters. I loved to experiment in the kitchen, and again, I felt close to Raquel doing the thing we always loved to do together. I could literally spend all day and night baking and it would seem like only an hour had passed. I loved it so much. It reminded me of a time when my momma, my aunt and I would all bake together, many, many years ago. Keeping those thoughts in mind, I made up a special "to go" basket with a little bit of everything I was working on. I figured one of the gals and I could run it over to Francesca and her daughters and made a mental note to make extra every time I baked for their family. I hoped it helped even a small amount with everything they were going through.

My momma, thus far, was MIA. She had not called or come by and I was relieved, but also knew this was going to be bad. When she did show up again, it was going to be because she had an army or at least some type of weapon at her back.

Sydney disappeared again. This time she actually took her stuff and left. She left us a note saying she would be back in a few days; this really upset Cabe and he took off as soon as I told him about the note, but wherever he went, he was back pretty quickly and seemed pretty chill...for Cabe anyway.

The third day after Sydney had left, I hadn't seen much of Cabe; we seemed to have come to some sort of unspoken division of duties: he on the wine and vineyard side and me on the events and baking side – which was weird 'cause it was exactly like my aunt and uncle had arranged their division of work.

We were preparing for an event for one of the real estate companies, which turned out to be a pretty big conference of about two hundred and fifty people with raffles, music, hosted bar and a silent auction. I decided to dazzle the crowd with a big three-tiered red velvet cake with my aunt's delicious cream cheese frosting. I was just putting the finishing touches on it when Cabe strolled in, sweaty and dirty; he'd obviously been out in the vineyards.

"I'm starving...whoa...that looks great!" he said, sounding surprised.

"Thank you – I made shaved prime rib sandwiches and put them in the fridge. There are four and I've wrapped them up so you could take them to work with you tomorrow as well." I walked to the fridge and grabbed one of the huge hoagie style sandwiches. "Let me just pop it in the microwave for thirty seconds."

"That's okay. I don't need it heated."

"It won't be heated," I said as I placed it in the microwave and punched in the time. "It will just soften the bread a tiny bit, but make all the difference." The microwave dinged and I served him his sandwich and a summer shandy grapefruit beer at the large island, where I was finishing up the cake.

He sat down on the bar stool took a big swig of his cold beer and dug into his sandwich. He started chewing, then stopped, looked at me and moaned.

Yes, that's right! Big tough Macho Man Cabe Brown moaned at the sandwich I'd made him. For some weird reason, this made my stomach as fluttery as a basket of feathers. And my body heated like I was dropped into a sauna. That moan seeped deep into my being.

Great. Just great, I was totally getting a girl crush on Big Man Brown. This wasn't going to bode well for me if I had to stand up to him about anything concerning Bellini Estates.

I busied myself with the cake and transferred it to the decorative wheeled cart I'd found in my aunt's pantry so it could be easily taken into the event. I could feel Cabe's eyes on me as I worked and he finished up his sandwich.

The timer for the latest round of brie bites went off, and I moved to take them out of the oven, just as Cabe was heading to the sink. We did that dance where he moved and I moved blocking each other's way, back and forth until he set his plate down on the counter, placed his hands on my hips and moved us both so we were on the side we needed to be on. I acted like it didn't send my blood pressure through the roof and hoped he couldn't hear my heartbeat, 'cause BOOM BOOM BOOM was loud inside my head.

"That was the best fucking sandwich I've ever eaten. What have you got in there?" he asked, as he watched me pull out the brie bites from the oven, hovering over me.

"These are brie bites – I am serving them with these," I said, lifting the tin, uncovering the prime rib skewers and crab stuffed mushrooms already on their platters.

Before I knew what, he was doing, he reached out and snagged one piece off of each platter and started eating my guests' food! "Stop that!" I yelled, slapping at his hands.

"Oh My God!" he moaned as he was chewing on the beef and then tossed a mushroom into his mouth. He kept chewing and moaning, and it was making it hard for me to think. It was also making it hard for me to move around, because he was right in my space.

"All right! I will make you a plate for dinner, but you can't keep eating these! They're for the paying guests.... stop that!" He snuck another one of the skewers off and popped it into his mouth and groaned as he chewed.

This man was a menace! He was going to eat all of my food!

"My God this meat is just melting in my mouth and the flavor is fucking *good*." He was staring at me in an intense way while he finished chewing, his eyes never leaving mine he reached around me to grab another brie bite off of the baking sheet and tossed it in his mouth.

"Stop eating all the food!" I said, slapping his hands again. He started laughing, dipped down wrapped his arms around my thighs and picked me up so I was forced to grab his shoulders or tip backwards. I looked down at him.

"Don't get mad, but your food is better than Raquel's and I thought she was the best cook I'd ever met," he said, looking up at me. His beautiful light gray eyes sparkling.

I wasn't sure what to do with this Cabe.

"I'm not mad. Maybe you can put me down so I can serve my guests and get paid so we can keep the lights on in this place?"

We watched each other for a few seconds, then he loosened his hold on me just enough to allow my body to slowly slide down his while still maintaining full contact. It was probably the single most erotic thing that had ever happened to me.

I could smell him and feel him as I slowly made my way to the floor. I broke out into a sweat again.

Jumpin' Jezebels!

I cleared my throat, "I'm not sure what's happening here, but I have over two hundred guests I need to feed and you're throwing me off my game." The front of my body still held firmly to his.

Holding me tighter, he leaned down to whisper, "You're beautiful; you smell good; you're smart and you can cook. Someone is going to be very lucky when you decide to let them put his hands on you."

With that cryptic message, he released me, grabbed a couple more of the beef skewers and left the kitchen.

Did he mean he wanted to be the one to put his hands on me? Or was he saying when some other guy was lucky enough to put their hands on me? I was so confused.

Later that evening, after the food had been served and the cake enjoyed, I was so happy it was a huge success: one of the servers came into the kitchen where I was planning the next events menu, and said a guest was asking to meet me. I'd stayed mostly in the kitchen and hadn't really had any interaction with our guests.

I took off my apron and headed out to the hall with the server. She took me to a table, where a good-looking dark-haired man rose as we approached, his eyes on me. He looked familiar, so I stretched my hand to him and as he took it, he said, "Hi Isabella! We met when my engine came out for the fire in the vineyard."

Shaking his hand, I said, "That's right, Captain Hernandez, right?"

Still hanging onto my hand, he said, "Yes, but tonight I'm just Steve."

"Thank you, Just Steve," I said and smiled at him, pulling my hand away. "I still have your jacket; don't let me forget to get it for you before you leave."

"I can come back later and get it. Isabella, this food is amazing; the prime rib is the best I've ever had and the little steak appetizers were really flavorful," he replied.

This was such a nice compliment I found myself saying, "You need to come for dinner when I make my BBQ. Californians don't know how to cook beef like Texans do," I smiled at him and he smiled back.

What a nice guy.

"Steve, who is this beauty you're keeping all to yourself?" a good-looking blonde guy said, approaching the table. He was probably closer to my age than Captain Steve or Cabe, who I assumed were both at least a decade older than me.

"Isabella, you should know Lance Drake. His family owns the Vista Rio Winery," Captain Steve introduced Lance and I.

Shaking hands, I said, "Yes, we used to sell most of our Cinsault fruit to your winery I believe. Sorry you didn't get them this year."

"Yes, well that would be my father who makes those deals; I run the tasting rooms, social media and show up at cool events like this to talk up our wine," he finished with a smile, a really nice friendly smile. I thought I could really like this guy; he was friendly and outgoing and something good just came from him.

"That sounds fun."

"It's especially fun when I get to eat meals like I just had. Did I hear correctly? You took over for Raquel and cooked all of this?"

Mentioning my aunt was probably normal since we were in her hall and it was her all around us, but it also put me in a weird funk that immediately washed over me. The men must have noticed, 'cause Captain Steve scowled at Lance and said, "Nice work dick head," put his arm around me and guided me away from the table.

"Lance is a great guy, but he sometimes lacks tact. I hope he didn't upset you."

"No. no. I still really miss them and sometimes a few moments go by and I forget, and then something brings me back to the reality that they are gone for good. It makes me sad again. I'm sure I'll find a way to get over it; or at least learn to deal with it, but right now it's still so fresh."

"Lance may be tactless, but he isn't wrong. That meal was the best one I've eaten in a very long time. It might be the best meal I've ever had. Everyone was commenting on it and they all had a chance to taste the appetizers in the tasting room too. Wow, you really have skill."

"Any news on the fire in the vineyard?" I asked, feeling embarrassed and needed to segue onto another topic.

"Yes. I just finished the report and will get it over to you tomorrow. The fire was probably intentional but structured in a manner to cause the least amount of damage to the vines. I think they were targeting the crop, not the vines."

He was talking to me while he kept his arm around my shoulders and had turned his big body so that he was facing me. For all intents and purposes, I was basically standing in his arms, when out of nowhere, Cabe came waltzing in.

"That's interesting. So, whoever set the fire wanted us to lose the crop, but not lose the vines?" I asked.

"It would appear so." Captain Steve saw Cabe the same time I did, and I could feel his body stiffen and he tightened his arms slightly. I got the clear message he wasn't going to be letting me slip away before Cabe made it to us.

Yet that was exactly what was happening; Cabe was making his way to us in big long aggressive strides.

"Hernandez." Cabe said, in a clipped tone.

"Brown." Captain Steve said back in the same tone.

Great. Macho Man standoff. There was no way this was going to end well for me.

"Wanna take your hands-off Isabella?" It wasn't really a question – even though it was framed as one. It was definitely a demand.

"No." I felt Captain Steve's other arm come up and around me too.

Great.

That's going to go over like a ton of bricks.

Cabe stepped closer to us and Captain Steve tightened his arms around me even more. I tried to lean back a bit to give some distance, but there wasn't enough room, and he wasn't giving an inch.

"I've just decided that I've met the woman of my dreams and I'm going to marry her," Captain Steve announced to Cabe.

"Really? When is this marriage going to take place?" Cabe asked.

"After we date awhile and Isabella here feeds me more of her amazing food," he replied.

"Good, then I have some time to convince her not to marry an adrenaline junky fireman who can't keep it in his pants," Cabe said, reaching for me.

"What can't you keep in your pants?" I asked Captain Steve, with exaggerated curiosity.

"His brain," Cabe replied and pulled me out of Captain Steve's arms. The Captain let me go, so the transition was smooth and the banter kinda fun, but I was still unsure what was going on with Cabe.

I turned and waved fingers at Captain Steve as Cabe pulled me out of the hall. I was rewarded with a big wide smile that reached his eyes.

I really liked that guy.

CHAPTER 8

Brothers and Sisters?

The following morning was busy, as we had two functions happening that evening. The first one was a smaller gathering in the tasting room and the second was a rather large affair: a rehearsal dinner for a wedding that would be taking place at Bellini Estate. The wedding planner was already on site and had all sorts of deliveries happening, creating an exciting fervor. I loved it. All of it.

Both kitchens were going full swing when the wedding planner contracted for the rehearsal dinner, and wedding the next morning, rushed into the tasting room kitchen, where I was rolling out fresh dough for the individual beef wellingtons, I was making for the rehearsal dinner, and Stacy was going over the evening's schedule with me while I worked.

"We have a serious problem!" she exclaimed. I stayed calm, because this wedding planner was extremely high strung and everything from the table placement, to the water level in the vases were "serious problems" and waited for her to expand on her newest issue.

"The bakery that made the wedding cake had a kitchen fire and everything is ruined!" she screeched.

Well now, I couldn't say I disagreed with her. No wedding cake at a wedding *was* a big problem; it was Friday, early afternoon, and the wedding was the next day. Wedding cakes were not super difficult unless they wanted a ton of sugar adornments or large unusual shapes that I'd need to make ahead of time.

"Okay, do you have another bakery lined up?" I asked calmly, moving around the kitchen continuing on with my work.

"No!" she shouted and actually stomped her foot: that's right, she stomped her stiletto clad foot and shouted at me, "I heard you made a three-tiered red velvet cake recently!" She made it sound like an accusation.

"Yes, I did. What kind of cake is your couple looking for?" I asked, knowing full well whatever I did wasn't going to be exactly what the bride and groom and most importantly, the crazy wedding planner would want. Yet I was not going to let the couple get married at Bellini Estate with no wedding cake.

"They booked a white cake with lemon custard filling – three-tier with white icing." Seriously? That was it?

"Do they have a topper?" I asked.

"No, they just wanted fresh flowers cascading down the side of the cake," she replied, starting to sound a little more hopeful. "I have all the flowers; I can stick them in the refrigerator in the morning."

"Alright, let me work up a proposal and get a signature from you, and I will get started on it." That's when the Crazy Wedding Planner really lost her mind, threw herself at me, grabbed me, squeezed hard, trapping my arms down against my body and screamed, "I LOVE YOU!" She released me suddenly, turned on her stiletto and ran out the door. The click-clack of her ridiculously high heels echoed off the walls as she ran down the hall.

I looked at Stacy and stuck out my tongue, making her laugh.

That was fun. Not!

After searching my aunt's kitchen for all of the items I'd need, I made a list of the things I'd have to order from the store. I liked fresh organic ingredients if I could have them and I was lucky enough to know my aunt always froze the lemon juice from her trees every harvest, so she would have lemon juice to use throughout the year in her recipes. She hadn't let me down, and with a wave of happiness that was immediately followed by a wave of grief, I found her stash of freshly squeezed lemon cubes in the small walk in freezer.

Sometime after the Crazy Wedding Planner, who actually had a real name, Stephanie, I had another visitor.

This visitor came walking in carrying a huge bouquet of red roses. It might be the biggest bouquet I'd ever seen and was in an exquisite crystal cut vase, the bouquet hid my visitor's face.

"I'm sorry, the wedding party is on the terrace; you'll need to take those out there. I don't have room for them in my refrigerator," I said to the unknown carrier, turned and went to the refrigerator to grab some eggs.

I heard a heavy clink and turned back around to see Cabe standing behind the humongous bouquet staring at it. "These were delivered for you." He didn't sound happy or unhappy, just curious. Okay, I could go with that; I was surprised and curious too.

"For me?" The only time I'd ever had flowers delivered was from Raquel and Antonio. "God, I hope they're not from momma," I said, walking up to them to search for a card.

Cabe held a small white envelop out for me. I took it, giving him my best stink eye, turned my back to him while I opened the envelope.

"I'm sorry I was so insensitive.
I hope you'll let me make it up to you with dinner.
Please call me - Lance Drake."
Whoa. These California men were fast. They didn't waste a minute. Of course, I had just come into a big inheritance, but Lance's family owned a much larger

winery than Bellini was. Maybe he actually liked me and wanted to get to know me.

Problem: no butterflies.

No flutters.

Nothing.

Bummer. He would be so much more appropriate than Big Brown, who was currently standing behind me emitting pissed off energy waves.

I turned back around and stuck the envelope in my apron pocket, then picked up the giant bouquet of flowers and moved them to the table and away from my workspace.

"Well?" Cabe demanded.

"Yes?" I asked innocently.

"Well, who the fuck are the flowers from?" he asked, not nicely.

"Why should I tell you? You're being kinda mean right now." I said, setting the flowers down on the table and moved back to the island so I could get back to the cake.

Cabe, having not moved, stood staring at me and then when he stalked around the island towards me, I had an intense urge to run, so that's exactly what I did. I could hear his bark of surprised laughter, when I spun on my heel and ran out of the kitchen through the French doors and out the back to the grassy area towards the river, with Cabe hot on my heels. I had no idea what I was doing; I was beginning to realize that running from a big macho alpha male, who just might enjoy the chase, was not necessarily the best tactic on my part.

Even if it wasn't a great idea - I still wasn't gonna stop; I could hear him breathing and feel him right behind me. I think he was pacing me and trying to make me believe I would be able to get away.

I was right.

Just as I rounded the bend to the other side of the roman style concrete stairs where we would be out of view, he tackled me full on and rolled me to the ground somehow turning his body so he hit and I landed on top of him. And without missing a beat, he rolled us so we ended with him on top of me.

Wow. That was a pretty spectacular move.

As impressive as the move was, I was now stuck under Cabe, and was breathing hard. I had no idea what I was supposed to do. So Cabe helped me out a little. He leaned his head down and started lightly kissing first both my eyes, down my nose, then around my mouth.

While he was showering me with soft kisses, I went completely still. His hands were running up and down my arms until they grabbed both my hands and pinned them stretched out above my head.

Shit. This was hot.

He kept kissing all around my mouth, but not actually touching my lips as he gently moved my hands together so he could hold them both with one of his large hands.

He reached down between us into my apron pocket, dug around and pulled out the tiny white envelope that had come with the flowers. He released my hands and stood up in one swift move, standing over me while I lay on the ground staring up at him as he read the card he'd retrieved from my apron. He looked at me, gave me a smug as heck half smile, tossed the card on the ground, turned and walked back to the house without saying a word or helping me up or anything.

He'd just played me, played with me like I was some little girl, like a big brother would play a little sister. I mean, I never had a big brother, but this is the type of thing I'd think they would do.

Jumpin' Jezebels!

It all made sense now, while I was crushing hard on him, he was thinking of me as a little sister. No wonder he kept moving me around and being so bossy, just like I imagined an older brother would treat his little sister.

How embarrassing and what a DICK!

This really hurt; he was so handsome and so totally sexy, I wanted him to see me as someone he could possibly be interested in.

In my mind he clearly wasn't!

I was going to humiliate myself even more if I didn't get it together. I was stuck with him, so I needed to be the one who kept things straight. He wasn't having any issues keeping things straight with me. He was doing just fine. He also seemed pretty skilled in all areas of how to work me and play on my crush. It was pretty apparent he knew about it.

I got up, found the card Cabe had thrown on the ground and fished my phone out of my apron, dialing the number that had been written on the back of the card.

"You got Lance," the male voice on the other end of the line answered.

"Uh, hi, this is Isabella over here at Bellini Estate."

"Isabella, hi, how are you? Did you get my flowers?" Lance asked.

"Um, yes that's why I'm calling, I wanted to thank you for the beautiful bouquet, and invite you to a homemade dinner here at the estate. What do you think?"

"I think you're cooking is amazing, but I'd rather take you somewhere I can have all of your attention and we can get to know each other." He said softly.

"Okay." I breathed.

"Tomorrow?" He asked.

"It will have to be Sunday I'm afraid. I have an emergency wedding cake to make and events to cook and bake for."

"An emergency wedding cake?" he asked, surprise in his voice.

"Yes, that's right. I can fill you in Sunday."

"I will be there to pick you up at four thirty, that work for you?" he asked.

"That sounds perfect."

"Great. And Isabella?"

"Yes?"

"I can't wait to see you," he said and hung up.

Okay – little flutters. Hopefully, they weren't left over from Big Butthead Brown.

Cabe pretty much stayed out of my way the rest of the day and evening. I didn't see him for dinner, and since I was avoiding him, ate by myself on the private balcony off my room. Saturday was so busy, by the time I had the wedding cake done and decorated, I was exhausted. I left Stacy in charge of the staff, serving the guests, and cleaning up.

I'd called my Aunt Raquel's friend Jenna for some outfit ideas, and at her insistence, headed over to her house. It was a beautiful old English Tudor style home that was as impressive as she was. She was all about beauty, and after spending hours with her I had a super-hot date outfit that would drive Lance crazy and let's not lie here – was hoping to make Butthead Brown a little crazy too.

She took me to get a pedicure and manicure. I also got lash extensions and some new makeup. I needed these few hours of girl time with her. We stopped by Francesca and the girls' home to drop off a basket of goodies and a cake I'd made up for them. I was sending food to them pretty much every two days or so. I figured it was the minimum my aunt would do for her friend. I wished I was able to do more for her.

After the visit with Francesca and her girls, we both felt a strong desire to shake off the funky mood and stopped for a glass of champagne at Stella's wine bar, Poured. We laughed, talked crap about everything and she asked me how I was settling in and if I needed anything.

"This. This is exactly what I needed." Was my heartfelt reply.

I told her I would probably be calling her more in the future because I felt better than I had in months. She and I made a pact to check in on each other and spend at least one day a month together doing girly things. But truthfully, I was hoping it would be much more frequent than that.

I played with her elderly dogs and decided I was going to the shelter, where all of the Women of Wine Country Tribe volunteered and adopt a couple of dogs that deserved forever homes.

Jenna was trying to talk me into a 6k run she was training for, but after my little sprint with Big Brown, I decided I'd had enough running for the year.

For some reason, I didn't share my feelings about Cabe with her. I talked about Lance, who she knew only vaguely, and I told her about my flirtation with Captain Steve - just not Cabe.

As I was leaving, I hugged her and whispered, "I love you. Thank you for making time for me today."

She teared up and hugged me tight and said, "I know."

I wasn't sure if she knew I loved her or if she was saying she knew I loved the friendship and the fact she was stepping in where the gaping hole Raquel dying left, I think it was a little of both. Either way it felt good.

I'd driven Raquel's sporty two-seater Mercedes to visit Jenna. I had the AC blasting and the music up loud and was feeling pretty good, as I was heading back to the estate.

Checking my rearview mirror, I noticed an SUV coming up fast behind me.

I really--truly was not ready for it, when the SUV came right up to my tail and rammed me from behind as hard as it could.

CHAPTER 9

Don't Shoot!

The SUV rammed into me so hard my head snapped back and flopped forward violently, but thankfully my seat belt kept me in place. The contents of the car flew forward hitting me, the windshield and dashboard.

I was stunned for a few seconds and panicked when I saw the SUV in my rear view coming in quick for another hit. I stomped on the gas pedal, squeezed the steering wheel and held on for dear life. I said a little prayer and hoped that because I was in a small sporty car, I'd be able to outrun the SUV. I wasn't fast enough - but was able to brace before the next hit came. This one felt harder and my back end spun out from behind me. I couldn't think at this point but could see the SUV was backing off again so it could come at me from the side and this time would be able to T-Bone me.

I hit the OnStar button and got a disembodied voice, "OnStar."

"Nine one one!! It's an emergency! I am on highway-twelve east bound and I'm being rammed by an SUV!"

I could hear a distant 'fingers hitting-keyboard' sound.

"I've got you pinged, and emergency has been notified. Rescue is on its way. Can you describe the car that hit you? License plate number?" the disembodied voice asked.

"Oh God! They are coming at me! They are......" I screamed as the SUV T-Boned me. My aunts poor beautiful little Mercedes spun around and around and ended up resting in the drainage ditch off the side of the road. I was so stunned by this that I wasn't really thinking when I heard heavy footsteps running up to the car passenger side and someone yelled, "She's still alive!" I swear I heard another voice further away yell, "Shoot her!"

Shoot me?

No.

Don't shoot me!

Why?

Why shoot me?

What'd I do?

I cried out as I unhooked my seatbelt and lay down sideways as far as I could over the middle console, just as the window exploded next to where my head had been seconds before.

My God! They were *shooting* at me.

They were really shooting at me!

I heard and felt several more, bullets hit the car and then heard faint sirens. Thankfully they were getting closer.

I wondered in that moment if this was the kind of terror Raquel and Antonio felt – or did they even know they were gonna die? Were they just driving along and suddenly they were over the mountain? Or was my beautiful aunt just as terrified as I was in that moment?

My dark thoughts were interrupted, "Raquel, this is OnStar I've stayed on the line and can hear the sirens."

Of course, they thought I was my aunt.

"DDDDid you hear them shshshsshooting at me?" I cried out into the car.

"Yes Raquel, we heard and recorded everything." That was the last thing I heard; I think I passed out. I awoke when I was being lifted straight out the top of my aunt's car. Rescue had cut the top clean off the little car in order to lift me up and out. They must not have been able to get the doors open. I became aware again as two very nice firefighters lifted me. I recognized one of them from the fire at the estate.

I smiled. "Hey I knnnnow yyyou." I slurred.

"You do?" he asked, carrying me to the street.

"Yesss." Why was I slurring my words? "You werrre atttt my uncle vineyard fire."

His head swung my way and I felt his eyes on my face. I wondered what I looked like that he would need to examine me so long before recognizing me.

Finally, he must have recognized me.

"Oh, shit! This is Cabe Brown's lady." The firefighter said to the other firefighter who was helping carry me.

"Captain!" he yelled, making my head hurt even more.

I tried to tell them I wasn't Cabe's, or anyone's lady, but I wasn't able to form any words, my headache was getting worse and I started to feel really tired again. I shut my eyes and that was the last I saw until I awoke in the hospital.

******

Cabe's phone rang while he was working on testing the final run for the security cameras and surveillance in the last vineyard. He'd told Antonio more times than he could count that he needed to upgrade his security, but there was always something else that needed attention first. So, while they were able to see the fire had been started purposefully, he wasn't able to determine much about the arsonist, due to poor camera angles.

Now that the security was finished and Cabe would be able to monitor it remotely, he felt ok about leaving the estate and Isabella without too much worry. He had his own business he had left his men to operate and was surprised to note; had been run well. However, he liked his line of work, and really wanted to get back to it, at least the day to day operations. Cabe planned to leave during the day and come back to sleep at night and still be compliant to Antonio's ridiculous requirement from the will.

That old meddlesome man.

God, Cabe missed his friend. He wanted nothing more than to give him a piece of his mind right about then.

Cabe smiled to himself, Antonio would have enjoyed watching the turmoil Isabella was putting him through.

Ignoring his ringing phone, he continued the testing of the surveillance system. He grew even more annoyed when the phone started ringing again.

Ever since the world found out he had inherited a portion of the estate, he had been barraged with calls from everyone looking to sell farming equipment, people looking to buy the estate, or women wanting to hook up.

Between that and his nonstop preoccupation with all things Isabella, he was on edge all the damn time. He couldn't stop thinking about her. And even though he had been feeding himself for the last thirty years, he was still drawn to her like some junkie needing his fix, food.

Her food.

Yes, the food was great, the best he'd ever tasted, but he knew in his gut he would still be finding reasons to see her with any excuse he could, even if she was the worst cook in the world.

As soon as he was in her presence, he acted like a Neanderthal. His feelings got all jumbled up and he felt out of control. He hated emotions. Especially these kinds. These kinds of emotions Cabe hadn't a clue how to process, and that made him mean. He knew his behavior wasn't helping his relationship with Isabella.

He went over and over it and still when he was in her presence, he fucked it up. Every. Damn. Time. He felt like he was on an emotional roller coaster ride, and the real pisser was; he wasn't sure he wanted off.

He was sick of it and was looking forward to diving back into his own company Security Deployment International. The first thing he was going to do was participate on a remote assignment...just as soon as he felt safe to leave Isabella.

His phone started ringing again, annoyed he pulled it out of his pocket to turn the ringer off. He glanced at the screen and saw many numbers, some he recognized and some he didn't, but the one that stood out was the Fire Captain's and he had missed five calls in a row.

Something was wrong.

"Yeah?" He answered.

"Cabe, Isabella has been in an accident. She's being transported to Harmony Grove Hospital as we speak."

Captain Hernandez didn't beat around the bush, which told Cabe how serious it was.

"Serious?" Cabe's heart was beating out of his chest.

"Last check she was non-responsive."

"Mother Fuuu...." was all Captain Hernandez heard before the line went silent.

Cabe hung up and cursed the entire time he ran to his car and sped to the hospital. When he looked back on this day, he wouldn't have one memory of the drive to the hospital.

The only memory he would be able to recall were the deals he made with the Man Upstairs to please let his Isabella live and still be in one piece.

His Isabella, because she sure wasn't anyone else's.

******

I must have been dreaming; I thought as I came awake in the hospital. I heard a loud roar close to me, and I tried to curl away from the angry animal but was in too much pain and must have passed out again.

The next time I woke up for a few minutes, there was some kind of activity happening in my room. I wasn't exactly sure what was going on but it sounded like men fighting. I must have been dreaming, but it seemed so real. My head hurt so much I just wanted to go back to sleep, so I did.

When I opened my eyes and saw the sun shining in my room, I knew I was in the hospital and I remembered what had happened and why I was there.

I remembered it all.

I looked towards the door and saw a heavily whiskered Cabe asleep with his ankles crossed and head leaning back against the wall, arms crossed over his chest.

He was so masculine and always so full of action, but in that moment, he appeared so peaceful. I couldn't help but watch him and thought there weren't very many people who would have an opportunity to see Cabe this way.

What was he doing here anyway? I tried to sit up but my body was in so much pain and my head was hurting, the movement forced out a little whimper from me, that awoke Cabe.

His eyes popped open and he stared at me.

"Hey" I said in a scratchy voice that didn't sound at all like me.

He looked disheveled and I'd never seen him at this level of disarray: black whiskers, crumpled clothes and his hair looked like he had been running his hands through it all night. It gave his handsome face a menacing look, especially with his light grey eyes looking so hard and cold.

He didn't look pleased. It appeared I might be in some kind of trouble with him based on the looks he was giving me.

I continued to watch him as he sat up and let his clasped arms fall between his spread legs and hung his head low, like he was trying to compose himself.

"I hurt. Everywhere." I said in my scratchy voice.

Cabe looked up at me so quickly and intensely I felt dizzy. He abruptly rose from his chair and came to my bedside. He rested his hands on either side of my head caging me in and forcing me to relax back onto my pillow.

"You really fucked up Isabella." He said in a low deep growly voice.

Jumpin' Jezebels!

I fucked up? Had he not heard what happened? I was lucky to be alive.

"I didn't do anything wrong!" I tried to shout but it came out as a scratchy whisper.

"You did when you got your ass shot at!" He shouted back at me.

"I didn't do that on purpose!" I whispered back.

"Doesn't matter. Let me spell it out for you, little girl: I have been to war, been in battle, watched good men – no - GREAT men - fall dead next to me, while I had to fight on. I've had to play bodyguard to beautiful rich fucking women who would let me fuck them any time, anyway, anywhere I wanted." He said, in that intense deep growl he used.

"What the…" I started, appalled at not only what he was saying, but also the way he was speaking to me.

"But I have never- ever- felt the rage or possessiveness or sheer terror that came over me when I realized YOU, pain-in-my-ass-beautiful-fucking-Isabella were run off the road and SHOT AT!" He finished on a deep loud roar. "You fucked up, because now I fucking care about that ass of yours and no one is fucking shooting at you AGAIN."

He leaned in really close so all I could see was his face. "You are MINE to protect and take care of. You hear me? Antonio left you to me to keep safe - he must have known you were goin' to find yourself in a shit load of fucking trouble. And here we fucking are, YOU, smack in the middle of a shit load of fucking trouble."

I was starting to feel like Cabe was blaming me for all of this, but seriously, I was an innocent bystander. I didn't shoot at myself, nor did I ram my aunt's car!

Did I ram my aunt's car off the road?

No.

No, I did not.

"This is bullshit." I whispered. I could not believe he was talking to me like this after all I had just been through. He was seriously pissing me off.

"And then it gets worse. I get here and you've got a fucking line of men all arguing over who was going to take care of you. What the fuck Isabella? How long have you been here that you've already assembled a mass of interested fucking males sniffing around after you?"

He was being so mean, and I promised myself I wasn't going to let anyone speak so horribly to me again. I'd dealt with this all my life. It was total bullshit he was doing this to me only a few minutes after waking up from being SHOT AT.

Jumpin' Jezebels! He was such a dick!

I reached over and pushed the call button on my hospital bed armrest.

"Leave." I whispered.

"What?" He straightened away from my face surprised.

"Leave. I don't want to see you, not one more minute. I don't want you at the house and I don't want you here at my hospital room. You are mean and I've put up with mean and hateful my whole life. I am NOT putting up with being treated this way ever again, especially only minutes from waking up in the hospital after being run off the road and shot at." My voice was hoarse, and it hurt to deliver all that, but it needed to be said. I was drawing the line now.

His face softened and he said, "Isabella."

It was too late. I couldn't move forward with keeping my promise to be strong and make my aunt proud if I allowed this kind of toxicity aimed at me. I would have to deal with this as long as my mother was alive in varying degrees, but I was not letting anyone else treat me this way.

"You're awake!" a nurse said, as she entered the room and came straight over to my bed. Cabe stepped back away from my hospital bed so she could get close to me.

"Can you please make him leave?" I asked. Her eyebrows rose when I said this and glanced back at Cabe as he left the room. "Honey, that fine man has been at your bedside for three days. He didn't leave once."

Three days! I'd been here for three days! My God, what was happening at the estate?

"I've got to make some calls. Do you know where my phone is?"

"Let me get a doctor in to see you now that you're awake. If everything checks out, you should be able to go home pretty quickly," she replied after she finished her routine of looking at the machines and fluid levels coming in and out of me.

True to her word, the nurse had a doctor in to see me within the hour; after a whole smattering of tests, the doctor determined I was going to be fine and would just need some time to rest and heal. I argued with him I needed to go home. He argued back that he wanted me to stay a bit longer, but if I continued to improve, he said I might be able to go home the next day.

If he needed to see me improved, I'd show him improved. I got my rear up and showered on my own, (after three days that shower was glorious!) and took my meals at the tiny table and chair in my room instead of the bed. I made sure all the hospital staff saw me walking around (pushing my IV stand with one hand and holding the back of my gown closed with the other).

Cabe must have alerted all of the ladies, because the following morning Jenna and Becca came to the hospital with clothes and what they could find of my purse. My phone was toast, but my wallet and its contents were fairly well preserved – enough that I could use it anyway.

Cabe didn't leave like I asked him to but stayed far enough away from me that I could pretend like he wasn't there, which is exactly what I did. I ignored him completely. He was like a quiet, broody centennial standing guard over me and the ladies who visited.

Once I was finally released, Jenna, Becca and Terra were dropped at the hospital so they could escort me back to the estate, Cabe actually drove us all but I was still ignoring him.

The gals had fixed up one of the downstairs guest rooms just off the kitchen with a private balcony for me, because I couldn't make the stairs. It was going to be some time before I would to be able to get up and down them. I was pretty banged up and bruised. Nothing was broken – thank God – and none of the bullets made it to me – again thank God. But I had suffered a pretty bad concussion and so I wasn't to be left alone or allowed to sleep for extended periods of time.

Jenna refused to leave. She was so upset that the attack happened as I was leaving her house; she felt responsible. Of course, that was ridiculous, but I liked her there with me, so I didn't fight her when she asked to stay. We spent most of the time looking at her YouTube channel and watching her do impromptu Facebook lives.

Jenna stayed with me until Sydney showed back up at

the estate and got me on the payroll and health care that was set up for the employees. If something happened again, I wouldn't have to worry.

One by one all the ladies cleared out, including Sydney.

I was sitting up in bed wondering what I was going to watch on TV, when Cabe came into my room and sat down on the edge of my bed.

Great.

Chapter 10

Not A Nice Man

Cabe stared at me quietly as I sat propped up in the bed staring back at him. Finally, he let out a big deep sigh and said, "I'm sorry Isabella."

Well shoot.

Those words were rarely ever spoken to me, not with any sincerity anyway. But Cabe? He was dripping with sincerity…. oozing with it actually. It almost felt painful for him, and I had to bite my tongue to stop myself from saying sorry.

Sorry to him for having to say sorry to me.

Jumping Jezebels, my head *was* messed up!

"I shouldn't have spoken to you the way I did. You deserve a fuck-of-a-lot better, and I need to learn to take care with you and your feelings. To be honest, Isabella, this is where I would normally bow out, but here we are, just getting started, so I am fumbling around like some fucking kid and it's making me frustrated and you're catching the butt of it. You've been through enough without me making it worse for you," he said quietly.

"Okay," I really didn't know how to respond to him. "Thank you." I wasn't sure what he meant about us just getting started, or what he meant about *'taking care'* with me, or even what he'd meant about usually bowing out. I was just gonna be happy he was gonna take care, even if I wasn't sure what, exactly, he meant.

He sat watching me and it was starting to get uncomfortable when he said, "It wasn't fair, me playing with you. I already knew you were becoming something to me, so I worked to keep you at arm's length because I'd prefer not to be involved with anyone. But I realize looking back, many times I couldn't stop myself from touching you, or going fucking caveman anytime you're involved – especially when I see other men sniffing around you and I'm already thinking of you as mine..."

My stomach dropped. What the heck was happening here? I nodded my head, too afraid to say anything and screw up whatever this was.

"I don't share. So, I'd like to ask that you make an effort not to see other men while we play out this little drama we've got going on. It works out between us, great – it doesn't, no harm, no foul. We figure out a way to work together here at the estate and navigate each other without making it too difficult. Sooner or later I will be getting back to my business, and it takes me out of town more times than not, so I won't be under your feet."

"Are you saying to me you want us to become romantically involved exclusively?" I asked.

"It's the only way I'm going to fucking survive this, Isabella. I can't stand the thought of another man putting his hands on you."

I looked at him, waited a beat, and said, "Let's just take this one day at a time. We need to find out what's going on with people ramming cars I'm driving with SUVs and shooting at me. Also, did you find out anything about Raquel and Antonio's car accident?"

"Not yet, but Isabella, I don't want you going anywhere or leaving the estate unless I'm with you. Can you promise me that?"

Okay, maybe things might just work out after all. I needed things to smooth out, not become more complicated. I wasn't sure seeing Big Bad Cabe Brown was going to be a comfortable ride, no matter how hotty hot hot he was, how good he smelled, or how shiny his dark hair was.

"Yes." I didn't want to get shot at again! That was scary and I hurt. I was going to avoid repeating that event with every part of my being!

"Another thing Isabella," He had my full attention.

"I am not a nice man. It's no secret, and I don't want you to go into this thinking I'm nice, thoughtful or will ever be sensitive. If you want something from me you are going to have to be very clear what you want. You can't expect me to know what you're thinking or feeling. I am just not built that way."

Jumping Jezebels! That was just about as honest as anyone could expect.

"Okay. Let's just get past the 'my life is in danger' part and then deal with our feelings or lack thereof, okay?"

"Okay." He replied. He didn't seem like it was okay, but I didn't have any other answer for him. "I have something for you." He pulled out a small jewelry box, opened it and took out the silver charm Antonio had made for Raquel of the old twisted grape vine, but instead of a bracelet, it was on a delicate silver chain.

"I noticed you weren't wearing your charm bracelet like the other ladies. But realized while watching you knead dough, that you wouldn't be able to wear it much, due to your baking and cooking schedule. I thought this would be nice alternative for you and you'd be able," he extended his arms to me and slipped the chain around my neck, closing the clasp, "to keep Raquel and Antonio with you all the time."

I touched the necklace laying against the base of my throat, and, with my eyes full of tears whispered, "Thank you." Cabe leaned towards me and rested his forehead against mine and whispered back, "You're welcome."

This man was going to drive me to drink, and y'all know how much this girl hates the drink.

That night I slept fitfully; my mind kept playing over and over, the voice saying, "shoot her".

I hadn't needed to tell Cabe anything: one, he was in the hospital room silently listening to my account with the police detective who came in to take my report while I was waiting for my release paperwork to be processed, and two, they'd all heard the OnStar recording.

Why were there people out there trying to shoot me? It had to be because of Bellini Estate. I hadn't lived an exciting enough life for it to be anything else, and also, no one had ever tried to kill me before.

And if people were willing to kill me, was Raquel and Antonio's car accident even an accident? I needed to talk to the police about this, as well as Sydney, and let them know my fears. Didn't Cabe say something about taking another look at my uncle's car? I needed to find out what was going on.

Obviously, I was in danger. And since I liked living, I wanted to do whatever I could to find out who was trying to kill me, so I could make sure and stay that way, living that is.

******

After Cabe's declaration to Isabella, he felt a little more certain she would not try to push him away. He knew it was dirty to play with her heart, but he also knew if she didn't stay close to him, he wasn't going to be able to protect her. After the accident and hearing the recording of the men shooting at her, he wasn't taking any more chances. She could be mad at him, but alive after this was all over and she was safe.

He made a call to Juan the forensic mechanic he'd hired to go over Antonio's car.

"Hey Cabe, my man, what's shaken?" Juan greeted.

"Seeing if you've found anything on the car?"

"WWOOOOWWEEEEEE did I ever! Whoever these poor souls were, someone wanted them gone in a big way."

Cabe's heart stopped. "Are you saying the car was sabotaged?"

"I'm saying this car was so sabotaged, bro, that even if they hadn't gone over the side of a mountain, they would have hit something – the brakes went first, but the steering was next. They just never got the opportunity to experience all the little gifts that were left for them."

"What the fuck." Cabe responded. He knew the accident wasn't just an accident, but he had no idea the extent these fucking people were willing to go – guess now he knew.

"Bro that's not all, I have a list of systems that were tampered with, including the driver's seat belt being disabled. I can email it to you, or you can swing by, up to you."

"I'll swing by – any possible indication of who sabotaged the vehicle?" Cabe asked.

"Nope. Whoever this guy is, he's good. Seriously good."

"I'm on my way." Cabe said and hung up. He felt even more justified for leading Isabella on. Keeping her safe was one of the last things he was able to do for Antonio.

******

After a week of bed rest, I was starting to get around, but moving gingerly, due to my being sore literally everywhere, when Jenna dropped off a new phone for me to replace my old phone that was destroyed when the SUV rammed me off the road.

I was setting the phone up when all of my momma's crazy texts started flooding in. She flipped back and forth from being distraught at her only child's bodily injuries and then back to being pissed off about the inheritance. I didn't even bother listening to any of her voicemails as they started loading into the phone shortly after I set it up.

Checking the dates, I could tell my momma's text tirades had trickled down. She also never showed up at the hospital. I didn't ask her why. But I am not going to lie, it hurt. It has always been hard with her, but she had a strong mothering way about her anytime I was sick or injured. It's like all of her maternal instincts only kicked in when I was hurt or scared, and those instincts must have been concentrated because they were *fierce*. It would have been nice to have momma bear on my side – even just for a little while.

My phone dinged with a new text notification. Thinking I'd conjured my momma again, I looked at the phone. The text was Lance checking in on me. I obviously never made it to our date, because well, someone tried to kill me. He wasn't mad and had been checking in on me pretty regularly, sent several bouquets of flowers. He probably figured out the flowers had worked pretty good for him last time. He paid attention and I liked that.

But I had basically committed to Cabe, and even though I really wasn't sure what I had committed to exactly, I didn't want to be someone who kept a nice guy like Lance waiting in the wings. I would not want someone to do that to me.

I texted him back that I was fine and would meet him for coffee in a week or so, when I'd recovered, and it was probably best if he didn't come around.

According to Jenna, when he had tried to get into my room to see me at the hospital, Cabe didn't like that so much, and he and Cabe got into a huge fight, probably leaving Lance with the correct assumption that Cabe had feelings for me. Jenna and I both thought it said something about Lance that even with Big Bad Brown after him, he still kept checking on me.

Another thing that happened while I was in the hospital was my uncle's brother Francisco and his wife had to go back to Italy due to another family emergency.

This upset them and we all were very suspicious of the timing. Not that I thought Francisco or Sophia had done anything, but I was suspicious of all the accidents happening around me, and more specifically, the estate.

Francisco hired a winemaker to take his place from the Napa wine region. What *I* would have asked was why there was a winemaker available so close to harvest, but I was in the hospital and didn't have any opportunity to even meet the guy before he was hired, and Francisco and Sophia left for Italy.

Sydney had been eerily quiet and didn't even show up when I was at the hospital, nor had she returned – Cabe said she was fine and had Roman to watch after her.

I was worried.

No one thought I needed to be bothered with the truth of what was happening, so I figured it was time to take matters into my own hands.

CHAPTER 11

Macho Men Multiplying

I decided my first action was to research all the wineries and vineyards and who owned what, and where everyone sat in relation to Bellini Estate, so I spent the week studying the region from bed with the laptop I found in my aunt's desk. I made spread sheets, maps, and strategized, while Stacy kept me up on the happenings at the estate - which was running great without me. The tribe took turns helping out with the scheduled events and some light baking.

After that week on bed rest, I was fit to be tied. I needed, almost as much as I needed oxygen, to get up and move around and there wasn't anything that was gonna keep me outta my kitchens.

With that thought, I realized I had already begun thinking of Bellini Estate's as mine. I needed to talk with Sydney about the trust, changing ownership, all the corporate documents and legalities, as well as everything we needed to switch over. I discovered during my research it was going to be a lot.

I had a solid plan and felt much more like myself. I called the wine tribe to my kitchen and prepared for them an amazing lunch of chicken salad sandwiches on freshly baked bread. I'd perfected the most amazing recipe of broiled seasoned chicken breast with fresh herbs from my window garden. My recipe substituted cream cheese and sour cream for the mayo. I knew they would go nuts over it – which they did. I also served a lovely chilled Sauvignon Blanc that paired beautifully with the chicken salad to loosen them up a bit before hitting them with my proposal.

"Ladies," I began, after they had all eaten and were on their second glass of wine, "as y'all know I have been run off the road and shot at." I looked around, making eye contact with each of them. I needed to make sure had everyone's full attention. "And that is just bullshit in my opinion and also not cool at all. It's also made me seriously begin to wonder if my aunt and uncle's accident was in fact an accident."

Jenna, Becca, Juliette and Terra were the gals who could make it for lunch. When I delivered that last statement, the women went still and set their glasses down in unison, giving me their full attention.

"I checked in with Gloria this morning from Italy, and found out their tank room had caught on fire. How can that be a coincidence? I don't believe it was; I believe it was set on purpose to lure Sophia and Francisco back to Italy, which left a hole in our staff, and conveniently enough, there was an available winemaker for hire. I want to look into him, start there and try to fit the pieces together. Cabe is having someone look at Raquel and Antonio's car, but I don't feel confident he will share everything he learns with me, especially if he thinks it would put me in any further danger."

Jenna leaned forward and said, "Honey, you've got our full attention. What do you need from us?"

"I need y'all to reach out to anyone and everyone who might have info on this new winemaker we hired, and the beef with the wineries and the old vine grape sales. If my hunch is correct, whoever this is has a long reach and I don't know anyone here, so I don't have those connections, but y'all do." I spent the next hour bringing them all up to speed on all that I knew from Cabe and Sydney.

When I got to my momma showing up at the will reading with Mark Sephos, Becca sat up straight and yelled, "Are you shittin' me?! Tell me you're shittin' me!" We all jumped and her outburst made my heart beat quicker.

"I'm not shitting you Becca! Geez!" I said, slapping the island top with my hand.

"I saw Mark having a heated discussion with Rafael on the way in today. It looked like Mark was chastising him."

"What?" I yelled.

"Yep. Not more than two hours ago I saw him and Rafael having a discussion, and let me tell you missy – Rafael did not look happy - not one bit."

I pulled out my phone, called Stacy, and asked her to find Rafael and bring him to me in the house kitchen.

While we waited, the ladies and I went over who could do what, assigning each lady a task that best fit their skill set and or social advantages, and I was not surprised how quickly we all formed a plan. These women were amazing. Every last one of them was furious that I was attacked. But they were beyond outraged at the notion that their stunning and beloved Raquel and Antonio might have been murdered. May God help the poor souls who might have done this deed, cause let me tell you, these ladies were spittin' mad and gunning for blood!

"We're going to need Sydney. Has anyone spoken to her?" I asked. They all looked at each other and made a silent decision – Jenna spoke up and said, "Let's try to get done as much as we can without bothering Sydney for as long as we can. She really has lost so much and she needs some time to find her way back."

Well, that was cryptic, and just as I was about to ask what the heck she was talking about, Stacy and Rafael entered the kitchen.

I could tell right away Rafael was furious – so furious he was visibly shaking and immediately started speaking loud rapid Spanish at me and all the ladies in the room.

"Wait!" I shouted. "Please speak in English so I know what's going on. What happened, Rafael?"

"*Sí, señora,* I work for *el Señor* Bellini for many years. He teach me everything I know about the wine grapes, *sí*?" I nodded my head eagerly in agreement.

"This new *enólogo* does not do right for the grapes. He's ruin this year's fruit if he's not stopped. And to have that *cabrón* tell me I have no choice or he will fire me! Who is he to fire me?"

Still not really understanding what the heck he was talking about, I asked, "First, is *el enólogo* the new winemaker?"

He nodded and said, *"Si"*

"Ok, now who is it that said he would fire you? The winemaker?" I asked.

"*¡No! ¡El cabrón is el Señor* Sephos. He was here talking with *el enólogo* and when I asked what they were doing and he *va y me trata como si fuera un peón, un viejo jornalero!*" He finished this last part off with a stomp of his foot. I basically got the gist – Mark has spoken to him like a laborer and not the farm manager, and he was seriously offended. Rightfully so: Rafael had worked hard to learn everything he knew and earned his status and title.

I reached out, taking Rafael's hands in mine, and said, "You will *not* be fired. You always do what's best for this vineyard, always have. I love you; I trust you, and you are family here. I love your loyalty to Antonio, and will never forget how much he loved you. Never forget that, and never let anyone else tell you any different. If they do – you come straight to me. Okay?"

His agitated body straightened with pride, shoulders going back. I could tell this was exactly what he needed to hear, so I said, "I want you to go along with whatever this new winemaker does, but do not let him ruin the grapes; you and your men watch him. I need to see what he is up to before he learns we are on to him."

"Sí, señora."

"Thank you, Rafael." He started to turn away and I said, "Oh Rafael, text me the next time Mark is here, have your men alert you and text me if any of them see him lurking around. I don't want him on our property, and I want to call the police if he is caught here again."

"*Si.*"

"You need to let Cabe know right away Mark was here." Jenna said to me. I agreed with her and sent a short text to Cabe saying just that, which resulted in an immediate phone call from Cabe that I answered on speaker. The call became a long lecture on why I, and the Women of Wine Country tribe, needed to stay out of the sleuthing and leave it up to him and his big strong Macho Man brigade.

My words, not his.

Of course, I disagreed with his take and that led to an even more in-depth conversation where he reminded me, I was just out of the hospital from being rammed and shot at, and, with that point made, I was starting to agree with him when Becca yelled, "Fuck that

girl! You don't need any man to take care of you –
you've got us and we will straighten this mess right out
our dang selves!"

At this, Cabe became even more agitated and
eventually hung up on me. Honestly, I wasn't even
arguing with him. I didn't want to get rammed or shot at
again; I was just worried what the next awful thing was
going to be.

I was trying to be proactive!

Jumpin' Jezebels! So much for a little peace on the
home front.

"Becca!" Jenna yelled at her friend.

"What! He wasn't going to do anything. Now he
thinks Isabella is going to try to solve this with our help,
so he will enlist every person he knows to get the job
done."

"You don't think he was already doing that?"

"Raquel and Antonio are dead. That's what I think. I
am NOT standing by and letting anything more happen
to our Bella! She is all we have left of them! We have
been dang lucky so far!" she finished and caught herself
with tears in her eyes. Becca, our tough as nails girl, was
scared shitless and worried for me. It broke me a little
to see. I looked around the room at these ladies, who
were my aunt's closest friends and now, were my
closest friends. They were all grieving and scared too.
Maybe it wasn't so smart getting them all involved after
all.

I needed to rethink this whole strategy.

"Oh no you don't. I know, by the look on your face, what you're thinking and it's too late to shut us out. So just get that out of your head. We would never forgive you if you went at this without us at your back," Jenna said. She looked around the room, "We all have our assignments: we stay in contact and fill the other gals in on whatever we can, except Syd and Francesca. They can be brought up to speed once we figure out what's happening, and we know they can deal with it."

Everyone nodded in agreement and we all went about our assigned tasks.

Mine, unfortunately, was texting momma and trying to weasel out of her what the heck she and her guy were up to. I did not trust him one bit.

Without waiting, I sent my momma a quick text and asked her if she was ok and if she was planning to stay in California or if she was heading back to Texas. I figured it was a good opener and would tell me whether or not if she was still in play.

While I waited to hear back, I checked the schedule for the next events and got started, puttering around the kitchen, gathering ingredients and prepping for the baking I needed to do.

I set my tablet up for viewing, located one of my favorite bakers who was doing a Facebook live to play in the background, and got to work.

I had several trays of garlic roasting in the broilers and a choice rib roast in the rotisserie and was just sticking some little puff pastry bites filled with brie, rosemary and fig into the oven when my phone dinged.

Thinking it was momma, I quickly grabbed it up and checked my text messages. It was Cabe and he was asking if there was any food. Like literally his text was:

'Foo*?'

That was it. No hi. No, I'm sorry I hung up on you. Just Food?

Men.

I texted him back that there was food and he could come in and eat in the house kitchen.

I took a French bread loaf from some of the loaves I'd made for lunch, out of the cold storage, warmed it slightly and cut it in thirds. I hollowed out an end piece and filled it with some of the chicken salad that was left over from lunch. Poured a glass of iced tea and quickly sautéed garlic, ginger, snow peas and water chestnuts with a little brown sugar and garlic chili sauce as a side.

Big Bad Brown's lunch was all set up for him when he waltzed into my kitchen...with his two friends.

Mind you, not just any ol' male friends, of course not, they were, of the Macho Man variety, all dark haired - broad shouldered, with thick thighs, and (not that I was lookin' or anythin' but it was hard for a girl not to notice), their jeans cupped and flattened in all the right places and showcased their assets shall we say - front and back - brilliantly.

They were two really good-looking friends who I'd seen at the funeral and around the estate helping Cabe, but not yet met formally.

"Wow it smells great in here!" said tall dark and handsome number one.

'Uh..." I started, and broke out in a panic, snatching Cabe's plate out from in front of him where he'd sat at the bar and started to dig in, fork in mid-air.

"What the...?" Cabe started.

"You didn't say you had *friends* with you! When *you* come to *my* kitchen to *eat,* you indicate to me *first off* if you have anyone with you. DO YOU HEAR ME?" I finished with a shout and stomped away with Cabe's plate muttering about poor manners and ungrateful men, and quickly made up the rest of the chicken salad and sautéed more snow peas and water chestnuts, stomping and complaining the entire time.

I set two more places at the island bar, shot Cabe with my best stink eye every chance I got, and ignored both of his friends' low laughter.

Finally, the veggies were perfect, and I plated them with the sandwiches, and tea poured for everyone. Only after I served Cabe's friends with a big smile, did I place Cabe's plate back in front of him.

I turned away, only to smile to myself when I heard the appreciative moans; this was my favorite time, when someone first dug into the food, I'd made them, and they couldn't hold in the happiness it produced.

"Ma'am, my name's Marcus and I'd like to officially proclaim my undying love for you and ask for your hand in marriage." The was from the Macho Man, aka hot guy number two, sitting furthest from Cabe luckily for him, 'cause Cabe shot him with a death glare if I'd ever seen one.

"Well, since you're the second man this month to ask for my hand in marriage after tasting my food, I'm afraid my response will have to be: get in line."

In unison the men, even Cabe, all threw their heads back and roared with laughter.

I thought it was humorous, but not *that* funny.

Men.

My attention was diverted when my phone dinged again and when I checked this time; it was my momma.

'Styn n cali u ddnt thnk ud get rid of me tht ezy did ya?'

Shoot. A girl could hope couldn't she. I texted her back.

'Momma, if you go home now, I'll sign the house over to you. It'll be yours free and clear. I will even pay the taxes and keep the lights, water and trash going for you.'

I held my breath waiting for the response, not realizing the kitchen had gone quiet and the men were watching me closely. Her text came back immediately.

'Whyd i do tht whn im gttn it all anywy '

Well shit. That was that. She was going to be something else to keep in my focus. My momma was mean and wily and was almost scarier than the men ramming me with their SUV's. Almost.

I looked up at Cabe and said, "Momma's stayin' in California."

"I know."

"You know?"

"Yes."

"You'd think maybe to keep me informed too?" I knew he wasn't going to, but it didn't mean I was any less irritated about it. "Did you also know that Mark Sephos was here today and threatened to fire Rafael?"

Cabe's body language told me that he did not, in fact, know about Mark and he didn't look happy about it. I liked that, so I continued, "And did you also know Mark was caught speaking privately to the new winemaker and Rafael says the new guy is going to ruin the grapes?"

I stopped speaking when I heard the loud front door chimes go off. It was weird, because no one but staff was around the house and they would know to come in this time of day. It also was weird, 'cause I'd never heard them before. They were beautiful, and loud, and...somehow, I knew I would grow to dread those chimes anytime I heard them.

CHAPTER 12

Momma Strikes Again

My phone, Cabe's phone, the house phone and the door chimes, all went off around the same time. I started towards the door but stopped short when my phone started ringing and Cabe's shortly after that. It was so much ruckus, I became a little over sensitized and it slowed my responses – I honestly wasn't sure what to do first.

The sudden commotion had Cabe reacting very differently than me. He immediately answered his phone, and whoever was on the other end, and whatever they said to him, gave him the info he needed to storm, in long aggressive strides, from the kitchen to the front door. I went to follow, but hottie number one (this one was Lucas) gently caught my arm in a loose grip as I tried to swing past him and said, "Go ahead and answer your phone *Chica*, Let Cabe handle whoever is at the door. If it's for you, he'll come get you."

It was said super sweet and he wasn't holding firmly onto me, but I still got the feeling I wasn't leaving the kitchen. Now, normally I would have had a serious attitude about this and given him some of my "You aren't the boss of me" sass; but I gotta say having your car destroyed by being rammed, and shot at, forcing you to be in the hospital for several days changes how you respond to certain circumstances. When you've got a couple of big badass Macho Men who know how to handle themselves offering suggestions of safety – well, if you have any smarts about you at all, you at least listen to them.

Which I did.

I answered my phone and it was Stacy, who was calling to let me know she had received a call from one of the recipients from the scholarship Raquel and Antonio had given out. They had been served with legal papers saying the will was being contested.

I was in shock. The house phone started ringing again, prompting me to run to the office/library to answer it. The caller was also a very upset employees' wife who had also received legal documents that said their inheritance (this time one of the rental homes) was being contested.

I knew in my gut what this was - *who* this was, and a cold numbness washed over me. Would I never be free of this woman? Would I never be able to have any kind of a life? Would she always be there to screw things up for me?

Yes.

Yes, she would. I knew it was my momma who was behind this and I also had a pretty good idea that her boyfriend Mark was knee deep in it as well. I was sure at this point he came looking for momma and I think he wined and dined and white knighted her, the entire time working to get her to fall for him on purpose. Which also then led me to believe he did this knowing my aunt and uncle were going to die, and this also meant he killed them or had the knowledge someone was going to kill them.

A cold shudder rocked my body with these dark thoughts.

Cabe came walking back into the kitchen furious, holding a package of papers in his hand. I could tell right away that this was not going to be a good situation.

"Isabella, you might want to take a seat," I took one look at him and I thought "Okay - maybe I wanted to take a seat."

Hottie number one and hottie number two both stood, and since their chairs at the bar where they were eating were vacant, I sat down in the closest one to me, "Isabella, your fucking mother is contesting the will; she's sent a fucking cease-and-desist letter and a contested notification to every single person who was in Raquel and Antonio's will, so right now everything is frozen and we can't do a fucking thing until this is resolved through legal avenues. Sydney was on the phone with me; she got served first and honey, this shit is not good. Her attorney is the Markin's attorney."

Cabe stopped speaking for a minute to gage my reaction, I think – or just take a breath. Either way, he stopped speaking and it gave me a second to start to process when he said, "Sydney is aware of this, their attorney is really, *really* good. No, he's a fucking shark, but he's a really good fucking shark, so right now we've just got to play everything tight and close to the vest, keep things going as if everything is normal, but we got to keep a fucking close eye on everything that's happening here at the estate." Then he threw his head back and yelled to the ceiling, "Like I needed one more fucking thing to deal with!"

I was so shocked that I couldn't really speak. I was trying to take everything in, and, to be honest, I wasn't sure how good I was doing coping with all of the things I'd been hit with. Since my aunt and uncle had passed, it seemed like I was on a game show featuring me and the premise of the show was to see how many hits I could take before I caved. My ears were ringing and I was sure my blood pressure had risen so high they were gonna be hauling me off to the hospital again!

I needed to calm myself.

I took a deep breath.

Then I took another.

Looking down at my clenching hands, I worked towards quieting my head so I could think.

I knew this was going to happen. Well, I didn't know this exact thing would happen, but I should've known my momma would do something like this. I am not sure, with everything I knew about my momma, why I was surprised. I didn't know what was more upsetting: that this was happening, or that I was surprised this was happening?

Why wasn't I prepared? I should know better and should be ready for anything she threw at me. I mean, seriously, did she know my aunt and uncle were going to die?

 My aunt was very clear about not wanting my momma to have anything. What grounds did my momma really have to stand on? *Everybody* knew how my aunt felt about my momma. What it really came down to was: I needed to know everything, I needed to know exactly what Cabe knew about my aunt and uncle being killed, and then I needed to share my beliefs with him.

My beliefs were:

One, that Mark is the one who killed them or knew somebody who would kill them, and two, he had made friends with my momma in order to be in her good graces before my Raquel and Antonio died.

So, with that in mind, I turned my body fully towards Cabe and said, "I need you to come clean with me about my aunt and uncle's car. I need to know exactly what's going on, I don't want any more surprises, if you and I are going to be partners whether we are romantically involved or not, you need to treat me like a partner, like an adult, and tell me everything you know, so my decisions are made with all the information available to me."

Cabe stood very still, quietly looking down at me with an intensity I'd not seen from him before, and said, "You're right Isabella. You do need to know everything that I know. I'll fill you in and we'll make a game plan. But right now, I want you to finish up what you're doing in here; Sydney is on her way over, when she gets here we will all sit down and talk about everything we all know, because you know stuff, and I know stuff, and Sydney knows stuff and the three of us have got to get a game plan and on the same page, alright with you?" Thank goodness. A game plan and a clear form of defense was going to be our saving grace.

I released the breath I didn't realize I had been holding and said, "OK, that sounds great to me. Let me just finish up what I'm doing here," and said more to myself, "The rotisserie is going to be cooking for a few hours. I don't have to worry about that. I'll get the brie bites out and clean up this kitchen and I'm done," and said to the room, "As soon as Sydney gets here, let me know and I'll meet you in the library. Now, I need you all out of my kitchen so I can finish up quickly."

I set about my work and the men left without saying another word. Actually, they both started to leave, spun around, and came back towards where I was standing. They reached around me, grabbed their plates of food and then left without saying a word. Whoever said the path to a man's heart was through his stomach was freaking right.

After I got the kitchen set straight, the brie bites pulled out and stored properly, I got a hold of Stacy and Rafael on a three-way phone call. I let them know that I needed them to take over, and that if they were served with anything not to worry about it, but to bring the paperwork directly to me. Once I finished with the call, I set about making a pot of strong coffee, knowing from past experience that is what Cabe and Sydney would want to drink, while I preferred tea.

Leaving the kitchen, I found Cabe huddled with his Macho Man group while they made a game plan for the security. They didn't hide what they were saying; which I appreciated, they simply laid out a game plan and it made me feel like I was on their team. Now, to be honest, I didn't understand seventy percent of the words they were using because they were using very technical terms about the level of security that was being installed like an umbrella over the vineyards. What I did understand was they had planned out a very in-depth security system with surveillance, that all of us would be able to use on our phones and tablets, which was very convenient.

I also got a phone call from Sophia telling me that she and Francisco had gotten served. They were also calling to let me know they had their vineyard and their winery in working order with Francisco's brothers (my

other aunts and uncles) and they were on their way
back to Bellini Estates.

See, I still had family.
Shortly after I finished cleaning and talking to Sophia,
the coffee and tea was ready and set up in the library,
Sydney arrived.

The three of us huddled, closed up together in my
uncle's library, and talked very frankly about what was
happening.

Cabe started, "I think we can all be very clear we
definitely believe that Antonio and Raquel, were
murdered. Their car crash was no accident. I spoke with
the forensic mechanic; he went over the car, and that
car was so tampered with there was no way they were
coming off that mountain. They're lucky, I guess, they
even got on the mountain. Everything, the brakes, the
steering, even the fucking seatbelts: I *MEAN everything*
was tampered with."

I started crying and silently wept as Cabe went on,
"There's no way they were coming off that mountain.
Whoever tampered with their vehicle knew about their
plans." He stopped speaking and looked at us both
intently before he went on, "So what I did, and I did this
without any of you knowing, was had the house swept
for electronic devices. And the house was infested with
bugs, *numerous* listening and *numerous* video devices.
We removed all of them. We did, however, keep a few of
the devices active out on the vineyard so we could
possibly trace back to their IP address. Unfortunately, it

was a very complex system, one that I personally would've used myself, which tells me we have experienced players we're dealing with here. Once the interior video and audio devices were discovered and disconnected, they knew they were being looked at, and whoever *they* are, immediately stopped all transmission, leaving us sitting on our damn hands."

He stopped speaking to take a quick sip of the coffee I'd poured him, and it struck me this was the most words I'd ever heard Cabe string together at one time. I looked over at Sydney and saw she was giving Cabe the tilted head look she gives when she is supremely interested in what you're saying and is hyper focused on you.

Cabe went on, "It's unfortunate. If I'd known that's how it was going to go down, I would've obviously done the removal process in a different way." He shrugged his shoulders and continued, "But this is the reality of what we're dealing with. Next question, do we need to have another look at Antonio and Raquel's bodies? I'm thinking no. We all know what they died of. They died because of the accident; I don't believe that digging them up and disturbing their resting place is going to serve our investigations. We already know the car was tampered with. We already know that the failed brakes and the seatbelt is what killed Antonio." Cabe focused on me and said, "We already know what killed Rachel. I'm sorry Isabella, we all know how and what they died from. We assumed it was an accident, but we know now that it was not; it was deliberate. Therefore, I'm advising we get Roman in on this case and bring him up to speed as quick as possible. Sydney, he's the best Harmony Grove has to offer, and frankly, it's his job and we need his help. From this point forward, we need to make sure that everything we do is by the book. My hunch is the Markins are somehow behind or at least mixed up in this, and if that's the case, there's no way we're going to be able to bring them down without the police behind us. We may still not be able to bring them down, even with the police behind us."

Sydney sat for a moment, looked up at me and then to Cabe and said, "I agree. Roman is the best man for the job. We need him." She turned back to me and said, "Isabella, you might not know this, but I've actually been spending quite a bit of time... in fact all my free time, with Roman. He and I are... I guess... an item. He may have to tread carefully on the case. I'm involved as a friend, but I'm also the executor of the will that is being contested."

Before I could reply that it wasn't a huge secret that she and Roman were sparing with each other Cabe said, "Actually I'm shocked Romans not here with you. I'm surprised that he would let you come by yourself, as much of a watchdog as he's been since you've been back. He hasn't let you out of his sight."

Sydney shifted in her seat and said, "Well actually, he brought me here and dropped me off. I had him go run and do something really quick for me, but he is

coming back. Oh, you might as well know. I needed him
to go get Agatha. She's been with Francesca and the
girls. We thought it would lift their spirits having her
around, but things have taken a turn for the worse,
unfortunately for poor Frank. Roman went to pick up
Agatha for me, and quite frankly, I've been missing her
so much. This is the longest I've been without her since,
you know. This is all too much for me to take in. And it
seems since I've been back, it's just like it was before I
left: there's no breathing room, there's no space, there's
no peace. It's like one thing after another and another
and a gal has to find her downtime."

Honestly, I didn't really understand much of what
she was talking about towards the end, but I knew she
needed us to just act like we did. So that's exactly what
we did (or at least I did). Cabe might know what she
was talking about, but either way, we both let it go and
moved on.

"Isabella, with Antonio's brother coming back, I
think it's safe for us to move forward and let the new
winemaker go. He's been causing problems and he's
making Rafael's job a nightmare. He's the one that's
been letting Mark onto the property. We need to get rid
of him. Also, we need look at everything he's done while
he's been here to see what kind of devastation he has
brought on." I nodded my agreement to Cabe.

"Sydney," I asked, "Do you think my momma knew
about any of this? Do you think that she knew these

people were going to kill my aunt and uncle, and do you think that she's been in on this the whole time?"

"Isabella, honey," she reached out and stroked my hair as she said, "I don't think your mother has the sobriety to pull something like this off. I think she has been a pawn in their scheme, from the very beginning. Now, does that excuse her free and clear of wrong doings? No. She still knows what she's doing; she knows she's suing for the will to be contested to take everything away from her daughter. She knows what she's doing to you. However, when she *does* find out, how she behaves will tell us a lot about how she's going to be moving forward."

Dropping her hand from my hair, she went on to say, "I better get started writing the response for the contested will. I also need to get all of the people who were named to sign off on letting me represent them or we could have an even bigger mess on our hands."

Sydney left the library to gather her things and call Roman.

Cabe got, up closed the door and came over to where I was sitting behind my uncle's large desk. I looked up at him as he looked down at me, "I'm sorry Isabella," he said softly, "I'm sorry this is happening, I'm sorry I didn't take better care of Antonio and Raquel. If I had even the slightest idea that somebody was going to kill them, I would've done everything in my power to make sure that they were alive here today."

"Oh, Cabe," I said, "I know you would have. I know how much my aunt and uncle meant to you. I'm upset about this too, but this isn't your fault and I don't want you to feel like it is. You just keep doing what you're doing and let's find out who did this to them and stay focused on what's really important."

He leaned down and rested his hands on the arms of the chair I was sitting in and said, "I'm not going to let one more fucking thing happen to you. I'm going to keep you safe and I'm going to find out who is behind this. This is no fucking way for Antonio and Raquel to be remembered."

Cabe caged me in as he leaned in close. Looking me in the eyes for only a second before resting his forehead against mine, he said, "Isabella I swear to you, I'll find out who is responsible, for all of it, and when I do, they are going to be praying for someone to save *them* from *me*. I won't let Antonio and Raquel's killers go free. And I swear, I'll save this winery for you." Tilting my head back and looking up into Cabe's eyes, I believed him.

I cupped his face with my hands and said, "Cabe, what I know about you... I know you'll do everything in your power to make this right. I'm not afraid when you're around. I'm not afraid at all. I'm free to be who I want to be when you're with me, even though I know I annoy you and even though I make you crazy. I'm free to be whoever I want to be, finally free, for the first time in my life to just be Isabella and I wouldn't trade any of that for the world. Well, that's not entirely true, I would trade my aunt's life for that. I would give anything to have my aunt and uncle back, but other than that, I wouldn't trade anything." With that said, I reached up from the chair and I gently kissed Cabe's beautiful mouth with mine.

I kissed him once.

Kissed him twice, and then he parted his lips and I went in for a deep kiss.

Holding onto his face, I lifted up out of the chair I'd been sitting in and he was leaning over, stayed locked in our kiss, and forcing him to stand up. I plastered my body against his, and as soon as my body fit against him, he wrapped both of his arms around me and pulled me in even tighter. He stood up to his full height and lifted me off the ground.

My hands moved into his hair. I ran my fingers through it. I fisted it in both hands in order to slant his head the way I wanted, so I could control the kiss, and slanted mine the other way to deepen this kiss I'd waited so long for.

Our tongues darted and slid against the one another in a sensual duel we were both going to win.

And....Oh.

My.

God.

It was beautiful, and magical, and my whole body was humming and alive. My fingers ran through his beautiful soft black hair and it was glorious.

Oh, Good Lord, this man could kiss!

The strength I could feel coming from his body through the kiss, his masculine beauty at play with my feminine aggressiveness was wonderful. Right then and there, I fell head over heels in love with Beautiful Big Badass Butthead Cabe Brown.

He slowly turned us around and brought me down as he planted his beautiful behind in the chair I'd just left and pulled me down, so I was facing him straddling his legs and sitting in his lap.

That was skill.

There I was, kissing Cabe Brown and seriously making out…. straddling him.

Dream. Come. True.

He had his hands on my back and then they moved down to my rear and finally, *FINALLY*, he placed his big hands on my big butt and then he groaned!

He shifted his head and moved his hands feeling up my rear, and said in a husky whisper, "I've been dying to get my hands on this ass."

And then *I moaned*, 'cause it was *hot*, I had to moan, and *then* we went even faster and hotter, and it seemed like his hands were everywhere and his mouth was all over my mouth and neck and ears and… Oh Lord this was the *best* make out session I'd ever had!

My ears were ringing, my senses were alive, my head was screaming about how amazing this man was. He was beautiful!

And he was kissing me!

ME!

Me, Isabella!

This beautiful man was kissing me, and it felt glorious, and it gave me strength, and courage, and I felt like in that moment I was the most amazing, sexiest, strongest woman in the world!

How could I ever be deserving to kiss this beautiful strong man? Yet, in my heart, I knew it was just as God intended.

Just as Mother Nature had designed in her most brilliant work, it felt beautiful and natural and perfect. I loved every minute of it. If only it could've gone on and on and on.... but alas it was not to be.

This beautiful episode of kissing; my first real make out session with Cabe Brown...hopefully my first and not my only... was interrupted when Roman and Sydney both came barging into the library.

Like they owned the place.

We tore away from each other as if we had been caught stealing coins from a church offering tray.

Well actually, truth be told, I tore away from Cabe, jumping up like a fool and wiping my mouth like I had done something wrong. I'm pretty sure they saw the way I was sitting on his lap and kissing him with his hands all over my rear end, but still, I tried to act like nothing was going on.... until Roman burst out laughing.

Jerk.

Sydney stood there with her hands on her hips staring at us both and exclaimed, "Well, it's about time you two! I couldn't believe you were still playing the game when I came back and you two hadn't done anything to relieve some of that stress! My God you two drug that dance out for a long time!"

Jumpin' Jezebels!

Sydney's speech was so embarrassing and forced me to break out in a sweat. I felt my face go hot and so I yelled, "Well my aunt and uncle had just died for God sake! What do you think I'm just gonna start making out with Cabe?" I flung my hand out towards Cabe who was still seated in the chair looking extremely relaxed and a little smug. I squinted a look at him and went on, "Well I probably should've just started making out with Cabe, but honestly it was not me who didn't want to make out!" I stomped my foot and pointed at him, "He was the one who wouldn't make out with me! I mean, he kissed all around my face one time after he chased me down and tackled me to the ground and got on top of me but wouldn't kiss my mouth! But instead my whole face! I don't even want to *go* into how he took the note from me and threw *it* on the ground and then ran off! Seriously, what is a girl supposed to do with that?" I said in one breath quickly, with my arm straight out and still pointing at Cabe.

Roman and Sydney just stared at me for a few seconds before Roman threw his head back and roared with laughter... again.

Jerky Jerk!

Sydney, clearly not sure what to make of what I just said, looked at me saying, "He chased you and tackled you to the ground? And didn't kiss you on your mouth?"

I nodded.

She then turned to Cabe and said, "You chased her down and tackled her and didn't kiss her on the mouth? What is wrong with you?"

Turning her attention back to me she said, "Isabella, I know this isn't very politically correct to say, but honey, I think we need to find you another man if all, *this one,"* (she used her thumb to point at Cabe), "is going to do is chase you down, tackle you, and not even give you one single kiss on the mouth. He clearly does not know what he's doing or has lost his game, so maybe, the cute blonde guy from Vista Rio Wines or that handsome firefighter Captain Hernandez, maybe one of them might be a better fit for you."

Roman, who had started to calm himself, doubled over, once again laughing hysterically at our expense over the speech Sydney just delivered.

Jumpin' Jezebels! He's a Jerky Jerk Jerk!

"Sydney!" Cabe growled.

I agreed with Cabe!

CHAPTER 13

Best Night of My Life

After that extremely embarrassing night of being caught in the library making out with Cabe, things got even more embarrassing. Well, let's say not so much embarrassing. I did get embarrassed... but it was more than embarrassment, so much more ...things got more intense.

More Cabe, a whole lot more.

The same night we got busted making out in the library, Cabe and I consummated our relationship.

After Sydney and Roman settled in with Sydney's cat Agatha into one of the guestrooms, Cabe took my hand in his, and we walked hand in hand to the room I was still using on the first floor.

As soon as we passed through my bedroom door threshold, Cabe had me in his arms and we were right back where we were in the library. Only this time it was even better; it was sexy and fun.

We laughed, we played. It was *all of the things;* you'd dream the first time would be with a super-hot bossy guy.

Yes, that beautiful strapping gorgeous man took me to bed, and it was the best night of my life.

I'm here to tell you when Cabe Brown puts all of his focus on you... you feel attended to!

That man did things to me, my body's *never* had done to it before, and they were *all* glorious and wonderful and made me feel special, beautiful, sexy.

If you were to say I could have a night like that once a week - for the rest of my life it would be amazing. To say I could have a night like that three or four times a week for the rest of my life would make me the luckiest woman in the world.

Cabe Brown is beautiful.

And skilled.

That man knows how to make this gal feel special.

Especially when he took *my* clothes off ...*goodness gracious*.... that's when the real magic began.

Big Brown has gifts no one man should have, but he has them. All of them. I think he's holding all of mankinds manly gifts hostage and I was thrilled to be the woman that he delivered them to.

After he stripped me out of all my clothes, I stood exposed in front of him and felt very vulnerable, but weirdly, it turned me on in such a way that my breasts began to feel heavy and my sex swelled and I probably had never been so turned on in my entire life as I was in that moment.

There I stood, naked in my bedroom with Cabe standing in front of me, fully dressed.

He was taking his time and the insecurities I've had all my life about my body were making the sexiness of the moment start to fade when he said, "Isabella, Good God, you're so beautiful." He walked in a circle around me, looking me over. "So beautiful .... I don't know where I want to start first."

I felt butterflies in my stomach from those words. He thinks I'm beautiful!

When he finally reached out, he did it with the lightest touch at the lowest part of my back just above my rear, "Should I start back here?" I was so sensitized waiting for what was going to happen, my body automatically arched into his hand. "You like this do you?"

I moaned.

It must have been the response he was looking for. He *finally* laid his large rough hands on me and I was gone.

I whimpered. Yes, that's a real thing and yes, I did it.

He stroked me, he touched me, he guided me, he murmured how beautiful I was and how much he enjoyed me naked, and he took me to places I've never gone before, and not once did his hands leave my body.

"I think I'll keep you this way. I like the idea of you being available for me anytime I want. Are you wet and ready for me Isabella?" He whispered to me as he dipped his fingers into my sex and slowly rubbed, the friction from his rough fingers bringing me to an even higher state of arousal.

As I said, I felt extremely vulnerable and exposed to him, but I think that was part of the sexual play and it was *really* working for me.

He removed his fingers from my vagina and stuck them in his mouth for a taste of what was yet to come, "Oh Isabella, mmmmmmmm I'm going to enjoy devouring you." He said in his deep growly voice.

I thought my legs would give out from under me.

After he examined my body with his hands, he started using his perfectly shaped mouth and began kissing me everywhere; he got to know my body, every inch of it, with his hands and then explored me further with his mouth, his teeth and his eyes. I loved the feel of his unshaven face as it scraped across my skin.

Anytime I tried to do more than put my hands in his short black hair, he would stop what he was doing and move my hands back to his hair, inhibiting my progress.

But I was becoming desperate to feel him, so I tried, I tried really hard to touch him; I wanted to explore and feel him. I wanted to feel his broad shoulders, run my hands down his flat stomach. I wanted to taste him and make his desire for me match my desire for him. I finally reached a point that I demanded he take his clothes off. Then I thought of an even better idea, and I demanded he let me take his clothes off. It was a little bit of a struggle that turned into a wrestling match, and that's where the laughter came in.

See, I was naked but Cabe was clothed and he found this very amusing.

Me? Not so much.

I went to take his shirt off.... and he resisted me taking off his shirt...actually made me stop undressing him. I pushed harder. He stopped me again!

He was literally fighting me off while I was naked. It was so ridiculous. I started giggling and he started laughing. The more we wrestled the harder we laughed.

Until we landed on the bed and fortunes turned my way when I managed to climb up on top of him. Since I was naked, my large breasts swung in his face. When this happened, he became completely distracted (typical male) by my breasts and leaned forward taking one of my nipples into his mouth. I felt his tongue run over my nipple and moaned, arched and slowly slid my hands behind me. He was super focused on my breasts and wasn't paying attention to what I was doing. It took some focus, but I managed to slip my hands down his pants and wrapped one hand around his erection.

Oh Goodness Gracious Saints Alive!

I struck gold!

Gold!

Once I'd wrapped my hand around his impressively thick erection and squeezed, everything suddenly changed.

Cabe let out a loud, "OH Fuck Yeah!" And we went from playing and wrestling, to suddenly he was very serious and couldn't get his pants off fast enough!

He was now on my team and we were both working towards the same goal.

A naked Cabe Brown.

Yay!

He managed to work his pants down where they bunched up at his feet, but he couldn't get his tight-fitting boxer briefs off in this position and got so frustrated he tossed me to the side, where I landed and bounced on the bed.

He jumped up, pulled off his shirt and hopped around while trying to remove his shoes, pants and underwear.

Of course, me being me, I started giggling.

Little secret I'm going to let you in on: men do not respond well, while they're taking off their clothes, when the woman who's waiting for them starts giggling.

Ladies, not a good idea. I made a mental note not to do it again in the future.

I must say the spectacle of Cabe hoping around working his clothes off made his muscles jump and move, all over his body and it was sexy. Super sexy.

Finally, he managed to work his clothes off and he stood staring down at me completely naked, fully erect, with a little scowl on his face. I abruptly stopped giggling. Not because of the scowl, but because of the nakedness. His masculinity was so intense it was borderline obscene.

His wide chest was tanned, muscular, covered in black hair and was one of the singular most masculine things I'd ever seen in real life.

I marveled at the sight of his flat tanned muscular stomach, with a trail of black hair going from his belly button leading down to the best of all…his large thick cock that was fully erect and pointing straight at me.

His thick, meaty, tanned, strong thighs were covered in a light dusting of black hair.

I've already shared several times in many ways how beautiful Mr. Brown is, but when he takes his clothes off – Oh Lord!

Everything moved very quickly once Cabe was naked.

Meaning me.

I moved very quickly once Cabe was naked.

I couldn't wait any longer. My thighs were wet, my breasts full, so full they almost ached from being so heavy and over sensitized. I climbed up to my knees, grabbed his hands and pulled him back to the bed, rolled him to his back and jumped on top of him.

Once I was straddling him, he placed his hands on my hips and grumbled, "Slow down Isabella."

Slow down?

Was he kidding?

After that statement, I basically threatened him, no not basically, I threatened him saying, "I will never,

ever, let you eat one more bite of my cooking if you don't put your cock inside of me...RIGHT NOW!" I finished on a shout.

I know that was kind of silly, but I was desperate and also it was kind of perfect, because he gave me exactly what I wanted, and laughed out loud while thrusting himself - all the way - into me, filling me completely.

We both moaned.

I broke out in a sweat.

I straddled him going still for just a second, and then I rotated my hips in a circulating motion causing his hands to grip me tighter, bringing my attention back to the moment, and with him guiding me, I started my sexual ride.

I don't think I'd ever heard Cabe laugh as much as he did while we were having sex. Gosh, I hope that doesn't mean bad things, but darnnit – it was fun and sexy, and I couldn't wait to do it again.

Did I say it was fun? Well it was. Totally.

And I rode him for all I was worth. He showed his appreciation by using his thumb to bring me to the best orgasm I'd ever had while I rode him. The orgasm started slow and low and built until it washed over me, creating a low sheen over my entire sensitive body.

My orgasm seemed to work for Cabe too. And if his yelling and cursing and growling was any indication, Cabe *really* enjoyed his orgasm.

That's how the evening went; once we were done and could breathe again, we stumbled to the kitchen, fixed something to eat, went back to bed, and had sex again. Only this time we used our hands, our mouths and our teeth, we explored each other.... fully.

There were lots of orgasms, little bits of sleeping; before Cabe would stroke me awake. We'd have more sex, and then we would end up back in the kitchen again looking for more food.

And repeat.

Several times.

One of those times happened in the kitchen, where we tried really hard to be quiet. In an extremely sexy turn of events; I must have been getting loud, because Cabe covered my mouth with his big hand; my rear on the counter, his mouth latched to one of my (by this time really sensitive nipples) him moving inside of me and with his hand over my mouth, I came – hard.

Hot.

Extremely hot.

I whole heartedly recommend it.

In that moment I knew in my heart I could do this for the rest of my life. I knew this was my guy. I just had to be careful and needed to make sure that Cabe was on the same page as me. Because otherwise, this girl was going to get her heart trampled on by this big bad beautiful man.

This sexual play, hearing his laughter, tasting him, feeling him - all of him, all things Cabe was going to be

easy to get addicted to and hard, heartbreaking to let go
of.

CHAPTER 14

To Date or Not to Date

All of the sex that first week really was a high point.

There were other things that happened that were high points but not great high points. Not great at all.

The week that followed the night in the library where Cabe and I were caught making out, and the subsequent sex marathon, was busy and lead into following weeks of even busier times. Harvest was beginning and momma was on her war path once again, only this time she had help.

Although the next few weeks after Cabe and I began sleeping together were busy, he always made time to have his meals with me (that was for him) and after our nightly sex-capades he stayed in my bed, and spent the night sleeping while cuddling (that was for me).

Several other things happened. We gave Rafael the approval to fire the winemaker and we recorded the entire thing. Cabe wanted to let Rafael have the honor of letting him go, due to Rafael having to put up with him the most. But Cabe also wanted to be there so he could protect Rafael if 'things went sideways' - Cabe's words.

Good thing too, the winemaker freaked out and tried to attack Rafael. Luckily, with a few of his farmhands and a couple of the Macho Men with him, the newly terminated winemaker never had a chance to lay a hand on Rafael. 'Cause let me tell ya, this guy did not go quietly! Whatever he was getting paid, besides what we were paying him, must've been a lot, 'cause this guy came after Rafael like he caught him sleeping with his wife! We were worried he was going to seriously hurt Rafael after he lunged at Rafael right in the middle of the firing process. His farm hands had to intervene, and the Macho Men brigade forced the irate winemaker off the property, like literally had to physically removed him.

A Macho Man had hold of his arms on each side of the cursing and kicking winemaker. He was told if he ever came back, we were calling the police and we would have him arrested. That didn't seem to matter much to him 'cause he kept trying to get at Rafael.

Finally, Cabe stepped in and told him we knew what he was doing: he was not working for us. He was working for somebody else and that he was there to do no good.

That shut him up and sent him on his way, but he was spittin' mad and shakin' in his boots with anger. The looks he was givin' poor Rafael freaked everyone out, so Cabe instructed the farm hands to keep a man with Rafael at all times, and alert him if there was anything that seemed out of order. Of course, the estate was bustling due to harvest starting and the crucial time they had between picking the grapes and getting them processed.

Apparently, after a little investigation, we realized there was a ton of work to get us caught up, as the winemaker had really set us back on our progress preparing for harvest. Rafael complained loudly and mostly in Spanish, but everyone knew how unhappy he was with the guy and how relieved he was that the winemaker was gone, so we just let him blow off steam; after everything we had all been through, he deserved it.

We were all still very worried about what was going to happen next. No one was under any illusion that the Markins were just going to suddenly back off.

Due to that, Cabe had his men all over the estate; thus, my servers were constantly stumbling all over themselves trying to be noticed by the Macho Man team Cabe had brought in.

We tried everything to get through to momma. We hoped, we prayed and then we tried reasoning with her. But there was no talkin' to her, so the next step was for Sydney to write a response, which she did. Then we got a reply from the judge, who set a court date and we moved forward. We couldn't use any of the bank accounts because Sydney said it was not advisable to access them until we had some sort of direction from the judge.

This left us with no operating capital, and I personally didn't have any money. Cabe and Sydney stepped up and provided enough money on a 'loan basis' to keep the estate rolling. It would be paid back by the estate once the court date was over. They didn't seem too worried about it, so after a little heated discussion between the three of us, I decided they were more adult than I was and knew what in the heck they were doing.

After all, once the court date was over, they both seem to think we were going to be fine and assured me there wasn't any way momma could legally take the entire estate and everyone's inheritances away. Every single person who was served by my momma's attorney about the will also signed off with Sydney, so that was good, and made things a lot easier for her.

She and Roman were doing some weird thing where they were always together, but she ignored him. I guess, from what I could tell, Roman was super attentive to her and seemed to take care of any need her or Agatha could have. He was never very far away from her, but she rarely paid him any attention. She acted like he wasn't there most of the time, until this one time, I saw him pick her up and march her out to the vineyards and when they came back Sydney 's hair was all messed up and her trademark dark red lipstick was smeared all around her lips. And also, I'm not gonna lie, her shirt was on inside out. She didn't know it and I wasn't going to tell her because, let's face it, I've done some way embarrassing things she caught me doing without saying a word, I'm certainly not pointing out anything Sydney does.

Seemed to me she was trying to fight with Roman. I think she was losing, and it also appeared to me Roman was really enjoying the battle.

We had another big situation come up. We found out my momma decided that she was already the winner of her contested case and decided she could sell the Cinsault grapes to the greedy Markin clan.

I was really coming to hate those guys.

So even though she had no legal authority to, she entered into a contract with the family to sell my uncle's prized grapes. They actually had the gumption to show up with a bunch of these giant harvesters, the same kind of harvesters that would never have been allowed in my uncle's vineyard, at any time. All of Antonio's grapes were hand harvested at night, not first thing in the morning with machines. The Markins knew this too – they were trying to rattle our cages and maybe they thought I'd give up and just sell.

They sure didn't know me very well, especially the me I was becoming, a strong version of me.

And they sure as heck didn't know Sydney and Cabe.

That morning, a huge fight broke out between our grape farmers and the farmhands who came with the harvesters. Another huge fight broke out between Cabe and Mark, who was acting as the leader of the Markin's harvest group. Of course, with Cabe being Cabe, and having his Macho Men on site, the fighting didn't last very long and Markin's men were all made to leave the property without too many injuries.

This really made me wonder what Mark was doing there in the first place. I just couldn't figure this all out and what his angle was with my momma: he had to know she wasn't going to win the lawsuit. All he was doing was making sure my momma wasn't even going to get the little house my aunt and uncle had bought us.

After the fight, we called the police and Sydney sent Markins a cease-and-desist and she also filed a request for a stay away order against their entire group, including their employees.

It had gotten so bad and chaotic at the estate. It seemed like everybody was fighting us, even though it was just the Markins. Our phones were always ringing. Sydney was super busy with her work and our events were booked solid.

I was busting my butt just trying to keep the baking going and sneaking kisses whenever I could from Cabe. I'd hired one of the bakers Stacy and I interviewed, and he was working in the event hall kitchen focusing on all of the pastries and desserts for our upcoming events, while I focused on the meals and appetizers. The help was much needed, but I didn't see how there was any way we were going to be able to do outside sales with us so busy. I brought this up to Sydney in one of the rare moments I caught her without a phone to her ear or Roman looming over her.

Handing her a fresh cup of coffee I asked, "Sydney, we're busier than a bank teller on payday with all of these events. I don't know how my aunt was going to do any baking for pickups or outside events. We are literally cooking from sun up to sun down, in both kitchens."

Sydney cocked her head to the side and gave me a small smile. "Sweetie, don't you know? Most of these events have been booked since you took over. I'm sure part of the allure is Antonio and Raquel's passing and the feud everyone seems to know about between the Bellini and Markins Estates, but honey," she reached out and gently laid her hand on my forearm, "most of the new business is because your cooking is so magnificent, that the word has gotten around. You're even better than your beautiful aunt – and she was amazing."

I was completely taken off guard by this information. Stacy and I had formulated a standard working menu and priced everything based on the items available per person, what area of the estate they were going to hold the event, and what accommodations were needed. I left Stacy to book the events based on the model we had worked up and we kept meticulous costing sheets on each event, so we were able to tweak anything that wasn't working right away. For the tasting rooms we had hired an acoustical guitarist who sat just outside the tasting rooms on the balcony; this allowed the music to flow into the tasting rooms without overwhelming the space, but also added a very nice *aviance* to the court yard that worked really well with the sound of the fountain, without inhibiting conversations.

It never occurred to me the events weren't returning customers of my aunt and uncle's, I just thought we were doing what she had always done.

"The event hall and tasting rooms have never been so busy; the changes you've made are small, yes, but that's the real beauty. Your return has been huge." She squeezed my forearm and said, "You're born for this Bella."

I felt like crying. I had been so caught up in all the happenings I never stepped back to see the big picture. I was just trying to survive, flying by the seat of my pants, and hadn't slow down long enough to take the time to see how far we had come.

After all this time cooking and baking up a storm, it was time I had a little bit of a celebration. I had been keeping Cabe and all of his Macho Men fed, and let's be clear, I was trying to show Cabe how good of a mate I would be to him, how well I would be able to keep him and his crew fed, if indeed he did choose to keep me around as a girlfriend, which was what I was hoping for.

It was a reasonable goal. After all I spent every night in Cabe's arms, he never left my bed once he'd entered. We spent our nights there together and I was happier than I'd ever been. Even with all of the vineyard and harvesting drama. Even with all my momma's drama, the pending legalities, the estate and the crazy busy days, I was happy.

There was one little downfall. I'd asked Cabe if he would take me out to dinner, on a date, away from the chaos and craziness, and also, I felt like if I was out with him, I would be perfectly safe.

His response was, "I don't date." That was it. Nothing more.

He doesn't date.

He doesn't share, so we're exclusive. But he didn't date? Like ever?

Does that mean he'll never take me out to dinner? Or does it mean that right now he's too busy to take me out to dinner?

I understood with all of the stuff going on, he just didn't want us out 'cause he would be worried it wasn't safe.

But I had a sinking feeling it wasn't that. I had a sinking feeling our relationship would be me cooking him dinner, him eating my food, and then us having sex until we fell asleep.

Would I never be able to go out for another meal unless I was with my girlfriends?

Ever?

These were questions that I was going to have to get answered. But I had to get them answered at the right time. Right now, it didn't matter so much obviously, with everything going on.

But still....

I could wait. But I sure did hope that he wasn't saying we will never go on a date because that would be really freaking sucky.

Chapter 15

Evil Pixies

Harvest was over and we had begun the wine making phase. It was super stinky, and the fruit flies were everywhere. The must (smushed grapes) were being worked and the winery was in full swing.

The last few weeks had been extremely busy, and I had not left Bellini Estate in weeks, and had the worst case of cabin fever ever! I needed to get out.

We were able to go before the judge, and after reviewing all of the documents for both Raquel and Antonio's will, he dismissed my mother's case.

During the court hearing momma was acting much different than I had ever seen her act before. I would swear she was sober, but it was like she was in LaLa land and was speaking by rote. I'd never seen her like that before. She didn't once look my way, or try to make contact with me, which was extremely unusual. My momma never missed an opportunity to drag me down and this would have been her prime time to do it with an audience and all. To me, she seemed to be following closely the directions given to her by Mark and nothing more. That in itself was out of character for her. The fact that this was the longest time she and I had been apart without her ending up at the hospital or in jail was also weird, encouraging, but weird.

With that over with, I felt a huge relief and I needed to get out for a while and see some people who didn't work for me or expect me to feed them.

The Women of Wine Country were having a fund raiser benefiting the Harmony Grove Animal Shelter the next night at Poured, Stella's wine bar. Bellini Estate had many of our wines there and a ton of the Macho Men were going to be there too, so I was hoping we would be able to go.

With Cabe's declaration that he doesn't date, I knew not to even bother asking him. I just needed to be able to get out and get away from the house, the estate, the winery and from all the craziness.

This was after a full night of amazing "up against the wall sex" where we literally made love, with my back pressed against the wall, legs wrapped around his hips and him, thrusting into me while holding me up. It was the hottest wildest sex I'd ever had!

Cabe found me the next morning in the kitchen. He told me he was leaving for the day and I was to stay out of trouble. I asked him where he was going and all he said was, "Got shit to do."

Something was off with him the last couple of days. The sex was more intense than ever and seemed to be getting more demanding and more – everything. I had never had a relationship anything close to this before, so I was fumbling around a bit and trying to stay really calm and cool and not let my crazy emotions screw this up.

Inside?

Inside, I was a mess of insecurities and doubt.

But then, at night we were as close as two people could be. But something was off, I could feel it. I couldn't pinpoint it and was too scared I was going to mess up what we had if I pushed, so I didn't.

Looking back, it would have hurt a heck of a lot less if I had.

I needed to be able to go out, and just be Bella again for a minute. I asked Sydney if I could go with her and Roman to the fundraiser and they seemed to think that was a great idea. I called Jenna and asked her if she would dress me for my first night out on the town in weeks. Jenna, of course, was thrilled at the opportunity and arrived at the estate with suitcases full of girl stuff. She used the time to make videos, pictures and a couple of Facebook lives, along with Instagram stories before it was all said and done.

It was all worth it.

I didn't even think I looked like me. I looked like someone else entirely, someone beautiful, someone worthy of a man like Cabe. It was just too bad he wasn't going to get to see me, and my new look tonight, but if he was lucky, I'd give him a private viewing when he got home.

Sydney, Jenna, Roman, Allistor, Steve and I piled into Steve and Allistor's SUV and drove to Poured. Jenna was my date, so I knew it was going to be a blast.

I was really looking forward to getting out; I didn't bother to text or call Cabe before leaving because I didn't want him to tell me to stay home. He was just bossy enough to do it and I was just wimpy enough I might – so I didn't give him the opportunity.

Jenna brought me a beautiful silver sexy dress that was stunning. It was brand new from her line and she was excited to have me wear it. I was excited to wear it for her. It really looked good on me, it was a gorgeous silver shimmery material and it went to upper mid-thigh. Loose yet clingy and wasn't super tight so it was very forgiving. It just graced my little buddha belly but didn't show that I had a belly, at all. It clung to my hips, and my breasts, and made my okay figure look like an awesome figure.

The straps were a silver metal chain that fastened at the back of my neck and then dropped down the open back. My whole back was exposed except the dangling chain. Anyone who looked could see I wasn't wearing a bra, but yet everything was covered, so it was uber sexy, without exposing anything. She'd also brought what looked to be the cups of bras with no straps that stick on your body and give you lift

Jenna really is the best at picking out what looks good on somebody. She could take a look at you and know exactly what you should be wearing. She told me how she wanted me to wear my makeup, smoky eye-nude lip, then taught me how to do it. She told me how she wanted me to wear my hair, big and sexy, then showed me how to do it too. I added some silver drop earrings, a sliver chain bracelet and wore sliver strappy sandals, grabbed a silver clutch of my aunts and I was on my way.

Steve and Allistor picked us up in their giant suburban and together we went to the fundraiser.

"Ladies, your men are so lucky I don't go your way, because if I did you three would be in trouble with a capital T. Girl!" Steve announced to us once we were all loaded in his SUV.

Jenna had dressed us, Sydney was in a red number that matched her lips, her hair was up in a messy sexy updo and was done, with a capital D from head to toe. Jenna in her signature black and silver was otherworldly in her beautiful appearance. She looked like a modern-day elven queen.

All the dresses were very sexy, and they were very ...very dangerous.

My thoughts wandered to Cabe. Was he off doing something dangerous or investigative work, or maybe some spy business? Who knew what he was doing? I just hoped he'd be home by the time I got there so he could see me in this fabulous over the top dress.

Steve dropped us off in front of the wine bar so as not to hurt our gorgeous shoes from walking on asphalt, parked and joined us. The band was playing their rendition of Brickhouse when we walked in.

What an entrance that was, us three - all decked out in Jenna's sexiest dresses, followed by the three men we were with, who were all gorgeous hunks. Every head turned our way as we walked through the door.

That is the best entrance music ever known to man and woman alike!

With a pep in our step, we all entered the wine bar. I immediately noticed many of the Women of Wine Country tribe were there, with all sorts of Macho Men standing with drinks in their hands, and leaning against the walls, like some Macho Man perimeter.

I felt eyes on me and thought maybe it was just because none of them had ever seen me dressed up as sexy as Jenna had me dressed. But I soon realized what was going on and why I was getting the looks. When I walked up to the bar and saw Cabe standing there with a beautiful little short haired brunette tucked under his arm.

I couldn't believe what I was seeing. He was there with a woman.

No, I didn't want to jump to conclusions. She could just be a friend of his or one of his Macho Men's wives or sister ...or uncle's assistant ... or something.

Jumpin' Jezebels!

In shock I went to where he was at the bar and stood in front of him.

I said, "Hey what are you doing here? I didn't think you were going to be around tonight. You said you weren't going to see me until tomorrow."

Cabe gave me a blank look and didn't respond and didn't move.

I was confused as to what was going on, so I stuck my hand out to his little pixie friend and said, "Hi, my name is Isabella. Who are you?" The pixie took a long look at me, starting at my feet and ran her eyes all the way up my dress to the top of my head and back down to my eyes. Based on the look she gave me she clearly found me lacking in a major way.

She smirked and said, "So you're Isabella?" and it was not nice, as in *really not nice.*

"Cabe, what's going on?" I asked, not understanding any of what was happening.

Cabe continued to give me that blank look and said, "Isabella, you're not supposed to be here tonight."

That's it? I'm not supposed to be here tonight? That's the answer I get?

"Is this your date? Are you on a date? A date in front of all of our friends, you're on a date for everyone to see? Is this the first time? Have you been dating the entire time you've been with me?" I could feel a cold chill wash over me. Everything was slowing down and my legs were becoming stiff.

"Isabella not now." He said coldly.

"Okay, not now. You got it, no problem."

I turned to walk away but turned back and said, "So let me get this straight, when you said you don't share, you didn't mean we don't share, you meant you don't share, so you are free to do whatever you want and date whomever you want. You just didn't want me to be free to date and see whomever I want. Correct? And when you said you don't date, you didn't mean you don't go out on dates, which is what I thought you meant, and couldn't quite get right in my mind. You just meant you wouldn't be going out on dates with me."

I raised my voice, my emotions taking over now that the shock was starting to fade.

Cabe dated. Just not me.

Cabe would be dating, just would not be going out on dates with Isabella.

"So, to be very clear, it's OKAY to sleep with me every single night this week, and to fuck me three or four times every night this week, and have up against the wall sex - THIS MORNING," I was yelling now and leaned towards him pointing my finger at his chest and finished with, "you won't go out on dates with me, but you, *are* going to go out on dates other people. However, I am not supposed to do the same, is that right? I'm to wait at home for you like a good little woman. Is that right Cabe?"

His eyes narrowed and his jaw clenched.

"That's what I thought." I turned on my heels and fled to the lady's room. I knew I wasn't going to be able to stomach whatever he had to say back.
I know it wasn't brave, but I had to flee.

I needed to get away from him before he and everyone else could see my heart breaking...no...shattering into a million little pieces.

I Stood in the restroom, my arms braced against the vanity and stared at myself in the mirror. Jenna, Terra and Jules came in and tried to comfort me. Jenna wrapped her arms around my waist from behind and laid her head on my back. It felt good to have her support. If anyone understood the devastation of betrayal, it was Jenna. I turned in her arms and wrapped my arms around her. We stood there holding each other as the other ladies stroked my hair and tried to sooth my wounded heart with their kind words.

They told me men were assholes and not to get hung up on Cabe, that he was not a one-man one-woman kind of guy. He never had been. I said, "It would have been nice to learn this before I handed him my heart on a silver platter. Would have been nice if Sydney had let me know."

"Oh Bella," Sydney said. I hadn't heard her come in, "I did honey, I told you to be careful with him. I'm sorry. I thought it was different this time. I thought he was going to do the right thing. I've never seen him so happy as he is when he's with you."

"That was happy?" I asked.

"Honey, that was as happy as I've ever seen him. Cabe is not, by nature, a happy man...Cabe is not, by nature, a nice man. But he's an honest man, and he's a thorough man, and he's a man you want on your side when shit goes down." She stopped suddenly and said, "Antonio and Cabe were the closest friends either of them had ever known. I thought it meant something to Cabe that Antonio left him to watch over you and the estate. I thought he would understand he finally had what he has been searching for. I didn't realize he would be so foolish." She said sadly shaking her head.

I didn't know what to make from all that Sydney was saying. But I did know disappointment and heartbreak. These two emotions I'd been dealing with my entire life. I knew how to suck it up and pretend everything was ok and that's exactly what I was going to do here. I would sort it all out tomorrow. I still deserved to have some fun after doing so well at Bellini Estate and I wasn't letting anyone take that away from me.

"OK ladies, I need a minute. I'm going to be okay; technically we've only been together for a few weeks. I need to get it together. I fell head over heels in love with Butt Head Brown in a week but in two weeks I can be over him. Trust me- I've done this before. But I got to get myself together and I need y'all to leave me alone or I'm gonna start bawling and make a mess of my makeup and it's gonna mess up Jenna's beautiful dress. So, if you don't mind, I need you all to give me a few minutes."

The ladies respected my wishes and left a pat, a hug or a "you got this" and a "we got your back". Terra whispered, "I'm going to give that little tart so many dirty looks, she has to shower when she leaves here tonight." I knew they'd be out there waiting for me with support. I knew for the first time, in a long time, I had a family of people who were going to be there for me. I wasn't alone. These women were my salvation.

After a few minutes I managed to pull myself together and left the bathroom.

As soon as I exited, I saw him standing there, waiting for me in the hallway just outside the restrooms.

Cabe was blocking the path back to the main room where the ladies and my support waited.

It was a very narrow long hallway where only the bathrooms and the emergency exit were located.

He knew exactly where I'd gone. He probably watched all of the women follow me in and then watched all the women come out before me. I leaned up against the hallway crossed my arms and looked at him and said, "What do you want?"

"I had a date set up with Jennifer for weeks. Long before you and me. I didn't want to hurt her feelings."

Seriously, who did he think he was kidding? He never cared about anyone's feelings.

"I understand." I said.

"Do you understand?" Cabe asked.

"Yes, I understand perfectly. You didn't want to hurt her feelings. How about Cabe, you don't do anything to hurt anybody's feelings? Also, why when it comes down to my feelings and her feelings, my feelings are the ones that are expendable?"

"Isabella, I warned you I wasn't a nice man."

"You knew. You knew I'd find out about this. You had to have known. All of my friends are here, everyone I know, someone would have told me. You did this on purpose."

"Isabella." he said softly taking a step towards me.

"No... no....no... do not step towards me, do not touch me, do not speak to me, do not try to chastise me, or try to talk me into feeling a different way than I feel. Nobody's treating me like crap again. I told you the night at the hospital, and I'm not gonna tell you again, that was your last chance. You don't get another. You will *never* make me feel this way again. I am *not* second-best, I am best. I *deserve* to be best, and I will tell myself that every night, and every single damn day for the rest of my life if I have to. To make sure I don't let anybody treat me the way you and my momma have treated me, do you understand Cabe Brown? Never - ever lay hands on me again."

Right at that moment, just as those last words were delivered, and it looked like Cabe was going to come for me, Captain "my freaking hero" Steve Hernandez exited

207

the men's restroom and started to walk past us saying, "Hey guys."

"Steve can you help me please?" I asked, my heart beating so hard and fast I could feel it in my throat.

He halted, turned and said, "Hey Isabella, what's up?"

"Steve, I need to walk out of here and Cabe will not let me pass. Will you please walk with me, to the bar, and buy me a drink or ten?" I asked.

Being the gentleman that Captain "my freaking hero" Steve was, he extended his arm. I took it and Cabe made no move to stop us as we walked, arm in arm, into the bar where I proceeded to get on my very first drunk. It was not pretty, it was bad and ugly, but luckily, I had all of the women, Allistor and both the Steve's who saw me through it.

First, they got me drunk, then they danced with me, Captain Steve flirted with me, the band flirted with me, and they kept me from being too stupid. At least in front of people, and when I did get stupid, Captain "my freaking hero" Steve packed me into Steve and Allistor's suburban and we all went back to their B&B where I could be stupid in a safe place that only my tribe, and Steve and Allistor would be a witness to it all.

I ended up staying at Steve and Allistor's B&B that night....and several nights after.
Now what the heck was I going to do? That man was living with me

******

The hardest thing Cabe Brown had ever done in his entire fucking life was to let Isabella walk away from him with Capt. Hernandez.

She was right. He had planned for her to hear about his date, but he never expected her to show up and see it. He thought they'd fight; he'd be an asshole about it and Isabella would know not to put her eggs in his basket.

Cabe wasn't a nice man, and the sooner Isabella learned that the better it was going to be for her ….and him.

What Cabe didn't expect was to have his heartbeat pick up, his palms to grow sweaty, and his stomach to form a pit.

He'd never had these reactions to anyone before and didn't know how to deal with them. He knew he was growing too attached to her and knew he had to do something to force some distance. He never imagined it would hurt him as much as it did …. or her.

He also didn't realize how in love with him she was until he saw the level of pain on her face from his betrayal.

And he certainly wasn't prepared for the panic that coursed through his body when she told him he would never lay hands on her again.

Regret wasn't an emotion Cabe knew very well or was comfortable with.

He'd done something he had made a lifetime career out of not doing.

Making bad decisions.

He knew with every fiber of his being he'd made a very... very bad decision by betraying her.

Chapter 16

Winemakers and Tummy Troubles

After the night in the bar, I spent the next three nights staying at Steve and Allistor's B&B. It was close to Bellini Estate, so I was able to go to the estate for baking, but it was far enough away that I didn't have to worry about running into Cabe, or even worse, worry about him hearing me cry myself to sleep each night.

That's exactly what I did – I showed up each day as the rooster crowed and high tailed it outta there as soon as my baking and cooking was finished for the day.

Sydney and Stacy knew where I was and were in constant contact.

You know who wasn't in contact?

Cabe.

Cabe Butt Head Brown was not in contact with me, not once.

He didn't text. He didn't call. And later, when I finally went back home, he didn't show up in my kitchen to eat any of my cooking.

I knew through reports from the staff, that Cabe and the Macho Men's security system was finally completed, and they had transitioned to monitoring remotely. Roman found me and showed me how to view the system on all of my various devices and sign in, if I needed to, from somewhere else.

Luckily, my uncle's brother and sister in law, Francisco and Sophia had come back from Italy just in time to work the grapes into must and start the fermenting process in the winery. Turns out, the fire at their winery in Italy was a small accident that got blown out of proportion because everyone was so hyper vigilant.

One great thing that happened: we interviewed a few winemakers and were very fortunate to have a female winemaker come in and blow everyone away with her interview. Her knowledge of the region and wine making process from harvest to bottling was extensive (Sydney's words, not mine) and, everyone really liked her.

Her name was Sloane, and she seemed to me to be very guarded. She had impeccable references and Sydney liked her right off, so we had her start immediately and set her up in one of the little homes on the estate as part of her salary.

Sloane was beautiful, no – striking. That is a better way to descried her. A striking woman. She had the lightest long blonde hair I'd ever seen, with strawberry blonde low lights, large dark brown eyes and brown eyebrows. Her eyes, in contrast to her fair coloring and hair, gave her an ethereal appearance. She had a small smattering of freckles across her nose and was a tiny little thing. She had all the right parts in all the right places and her parts were correctly proportioned to her frame, but she was so small.

As petite as she looked, I thought she couldn't lift a feather, but she ended up being crazy strong and extremely active. She ran circles around the guys who worked in her department with her. Not to be outdone by a tiny woman who looked like a fairy princess, all the guys picked up their pace and got moving. They were having a heck of a time keeping up. It was funny to watch and gave me the warm fuzzies to know a tiny fair gal could still wreak havoc on a bunch of rugged farm hands.

The women really liked Sloane, and even though she had a secretive nature and a past that she wouldn't talk much about, she fit in really well with the wine country tribe. It was nice for us and probably even nicer for her. Little did she know with this group; her secretive nature would only make us more curious and cause us to dig into her background further.

My attempts to avoid Cabe seemed to pay off, as I didn't see him for a couple of weeks after the bar incident.

Sydney told me Cabe was working with Roman on Raquel and Antonio's car, they knew it had been tampered with, and were now ruling it as a homicide.

Mark Sephos was the number one suspect, but we couldn't place him in California at the same time as my aunt and uncle's car wreck, because he was with me and my mother in Texas.

Then I remembered that my momma and Mark had made an impromptu quick trip out of Texas and were gone for a little bit of time, but then came right back. I didn't think anything of it as my momma would accompany Mark on weekend trips, or a few day, or overnight trips while they were dating. I wasn't sure if this information would put Mark and my momma in California around the time that my aunt and uncle's car was sabotaged, but the information gave Roman and Cabe an area to focus on.

They still didn't have anything to tie Mark Sephos to the accident, but they were digging, and they were digging hard. I had not had any more attempts on my life, but I was still under strict security protocols.

Twice I text my momma, but both times I got no response back. This was very unusual for my mom, because she never missed an opportunity to strike out at me even through text messaging.

Captain Hernandez became a regular fixture over the next couple of weeks, especially in my kitchen. He showed up just in time for lunch and then would come back around in time for dinner. A couple of those times I packed him lunches and sent them off with him the night before, so he would have something to hold him over if he couldn't get to my kitchen for lunch the next day.

He was sweet, kind, playful, and funny, and treated me more like a big brother would a sister than a date or someone he would be romantically interested in. But I thought that about Cabe too, so maybe I wasn't the best at reading men and their intentions.

Either way, he was a very nice distraction who kept my mind occupied on something other than Cabe.

Captain Steve didn't ask to take me out, and he never tried to kiss me, or touch me in any romantic way, or do anything more than give me a hug as he left at the end of the evening. I didn't know if he was biding his time to give me room to heal my broken heart, or if he was just keeping an eye on me to keep me safe. I was starting to wonder if it wasn't more the second than the first.

I knew one thing for sure, he really liked the way I cooked, and it was nice to have somebody to eat meals with. He would show up in my kitchen at lunch and sit at my island while I was baking and cooking for the events and then he would come at night and we would sit out on my patio under the stars and have a grilled dinner with a lovely wine or maybe a beer and just talk about the day.

This was something I could get used to. There was an easy, comfortable and relaxing energy about him. Same with conversation, it was easy. I didn't have to put on airs or worry, and there was no pressure to be anything other than me when we talked about our day.

We settled into a nice routine with Sloane and Antonio's brother Francisco working the winery, Rafael and his men put the vineyards to bed. Our new baker, Doug, and Stacy and I, along with support staff worked the event halls and tasting rooms.

Sydney occasionally showed up, but never stayed long. I honestly didn't know what she was up to and if I asked, she would act all cagey about it, so I stopped bothering her. I did let her know I was there for her if she needed anything – which resulted in a tight hug from her.

Weird.

As things seemed to relax a little bit around the estate, the Macho Men were in and out, but still around. It seemed there was always somebody at the estate from the Macho Man group, but Cabe was rarely, if ever.

On one of those routine days, a couple weeks after the bar incident, Lance Drake showed up at the winery to attend one of the events. We were short staffed that day, so I was helping to get the buffet set up and was out on the floor in the event hall when he approached me. "Hi Isabella, it's been so long since I've seen you," he said, giving me a brief hug and then looked around, "Is Cabe going to come up and harass me for talking to you?"

"Not any time soon Lance. I don't think we're gonna have to worry about that," I muttered, "like ever again."

"Oh good! Well, I can't say that makes me unhappy." He smiled at me. "So, what do you say Isabella? Think we could finally have that date we never went on?"

"I don't know Lance, let me see how this next week schedules out." I looked at him and watched him deflate a little. I felt bad, so went on to say, "There're a few things that, as you can imagine, have made me a little bit security conscious. So, while I would like to go out on a date with you, and I really wouldn't mind having dinner with you, if we did have a date, I think it would need to be here at the winery."

"I have an idea. Why don't you come over to my winery and let me make dinner for you over there?"

"I think if I went over to your winery to have dinner, I would have to bring the Macho Men brigade with me, and to be honest, I'm a little burned out on all the testosterone, so if you'd like to have dinner with me in the next couple o' weeks, let's pick a day and you can come here and we'll have a nice light hearted dinner outside on the courtyard and we can listen to the music and the fountain."

I was getting a little tired of trying to navigate Lance, so when he responded with, "You know Isabella, doesn't sound like I have much of a choice. I'd rather have dinner with you here then not have dinner with you at all. What day looks good for you?" I was relieved.

"How does Thursday evening sound? Around seven?"

"Thursday evening at seven sounds perfect. I'll be here."

I wasn't feeling like having dinner with any man except Captain Steve, but I also knew it was good to have a distraction and keep myself busy and dinner with Lance was going to do just that.

The rest of the week flew by, and before I knew it, Thursday rolled around. I prepared a beautiful roasted rosemary chicken with small colorful potatoes, carrots, celery and turnips with fresh baked biscuits and gravy. I paired this with a lovely IPA from Jenna's son's microbrewery, which was a perfect combination with the chicken. For dessert, I prepared my aunt's lemon raspberry tart and paired that with a freshly made lemon martini. I set the dinner up on the patio off the house kitchen and set flameless candles all around to add a little bit of romance.

I wore a soft pink tank maxi dress made from a light weight tee-shirt material. I'd left my hair down and full, and I'd applied very light makeup. It was a very romantic scene, and I felt pretty, but it made me a bit sad, because I was so not feeling it with Lance - at all. No matter how hard I tried. And believe me – I tried – hard.

Lance was an impressive date – he brought a beautiful bouquet of colorful flowers and looked very handsome. He wore a pair of light khaki slacks with a white polo shirt and was impeccably groomed with impeccable manners. He smelled good, looked good and was the perfect gentleman.

So why couldn't I feel anything for him?

I tried very hard not to let my lack of interest show, but I think Lance caught on, and finished the date shortly after dessert was served. He gave me a sweet kiss on the cheek, a promise to 'do this again' and then he showed himself out.

I think he left disappointed.

I noticed as the days went on, and the weeks went by, my energy level seemed to be less and less. I was needing more and more sleep. Then I came down with a silly little tummy flu. The smells from the kitchen really intensified and had me running to the restroom to get rid of whatever I had eaten previously – and then I would be fine, until the next wave came over me.

Whatever was going on with me, I was going to need to see a doctor pretty soon if it didn't pass. I couldn't be sick and preparing everyone's food and I couldn't work if I was getting sick every time a smell hit me wrong.

CHAPTER 17

Guns and Galas

For the next six weeks, while I nursed my broken heart, the Women of Wine Country tribe planned, plotted and executed another large fundraising extravaganza benefiting the Harmony Grove Animal Shelter. This fund raiser was one of many, and we were working on raising enough money to build a new shelter for Becca's rescue that would eventually become a no kill shelter. Becca would run both the shelter and rescue as the director and we all would take turns serving on the board.

This new shelter would serve as an overflow for Harmony Grove Animal Shelter and would give Becca the ability to pull from other shelters too, specifically, high kill shelters. The Women of Wine Country tribe had been working on this for years and it was not an easy feat, but the harder they worked and the more traction they got, the more attention people paid. It really was a beautiful thing to see so many come together and donate so generously for animals who were homeless and in need.

The event was being held at Bellini Estates and everyone was invited. And when I say everyone, I mean everyone: Municipal Advisory Council members, District Supervisors, and Fire District Board Members. We had a California Senator coming, various business owners and the local news media covering the event, in addition to the social media celebrities and influencers of the area.

We planned a black-tie formal affair set in a Rio de Janeiro Carnival theme, so people were wearing very intricate head-wear and their fanciest attire.

We decided to use Stephanie (aka 'crazy wedding planner') as our event coordinator. Yes, she was super high strung, but really good at her job, and we liked her vision for the event.

She did not let us down.

Everything was decorated gorgeously with beautiful beads, feathers, pearls and crystals in gold, silver, black, blue, green and red. The whole affair was opulent and colorful. I liked the way she had decorated the long table, with beautiful large sprays of white flowers. She'd even brought in giant potted trees that she had strung with warm amber white lights, so that the chandeliers had something to hang from. Our staff also strung a variety of lights in every tree, bush, and along the staircases. Six large chandeliers holding candles hung low over the center of the tables, and more candles floated in the fountain.

My team and I worked on the food for two days; prime rib dinner with all the typical fixings, served on the large beautifully laid table outside in the courtyard that sat one hundred, family style.

The table my food went on was the most beautiful thing I'd ever seen. The chandeliers dripped with crystals that reflected the candlelight brilliantly and cast twinkling light all over the table.

The candlelight also reflected off the highly polished sterling silver cutlery, the crystal goblets and fine bone ivory china.

The opulence was dazzling.

We all worked very hard to make this stunning gala happen and each plate sold for one thousand dollars. Without a doubt it was the biggest event we had so far, and we felt like we were almost halfway to the amount that we needed to get that first building up. We were all so proud that our group could pull it off.

Captain Hernandez was working that evening. So, while he was going to be at the estate, he was on duty with the other firefighters hosting a booth, as were our local CHP and our local Sheriff, the local hospital, Boy Scouts, Girl Scouts and the Harmony Grove animal shelter officers.

One of our local architects made a 3-D image mockup of the final buildings and it was really something. We were only tackling one building at a time, but seeing the full vision got everyone excited.

We invited Vista Rio winery, Lance's winery, to attend, as well as eight of the other neighboring smaller boutique wineries to pour their wines. We set up makeshift wine tasting stations around the estate. There were tons to do and it was very organized; music in one area, silent auction in another, darts and billiards with a draft beer station set up and hosted by Jenna's sons' establishment; Harmony Grove Microbrewery. We worked hard to cover all of the bases; we wanted everyone who attended to be wowed.

Every item was donated, so every dime earned went directly to the Harmony Grove Animal Shelter fundraising event.

There were over two hundred and fifty guests who bought drink and appetizer tickets at two hundred dollars each. Those guests would be able to enjoy the tasting rooms, music, games and other amenities and allowed entry once the dinner was finished and acknowledgements awarded.

I had been extremely tired the last few weeks. My little tummy flu had gone away, thankfully, and I also seemed to be losing a little bit of weight. That was a super nice surprise. I guess it all made sense; I had been working harder and longer than I ever had before, so that's why I was so tired. The stomach flu on top of that would explain why I was thinner.

Jenna, being extremely generous, and also using this function to debut her new formal line; outfitted all of us girls in pearl white and champagne beaded gowns that were strapless, form fitted and flowed to the floor. All of them were similar - but none of them exactly the same. My dress was a fitted, beaded strapless number with a mermaid skirt. It had pearls and rhinestones all over it, and was, to put it mildly: Shut. Your. Mouth. Gorgeous.

As Jenna instructed, (when Jenna instructed, you did! Seriously, the lady knew her stuff) I had my hair up in a beautiful complicated up-do with little bits flowing down from everywhere. I wore pearl stud earrings, a pearl choker with a beautiful pearl cuff that Jenna gifted to all of us, along with a sweet little silver heart with a paw-print for our charm bracelets.

She outfitted Steve and Allistor in black tuxes with beautiful beaded ties and pearl cuff links. They were both given beautiful head pieces that matched their extravagant ties. Stella teared up as Jenna was presenting the cuff links to the guys and said, "Raquel would be so happy to see this - how far we've come and what we have accomplished...I miss her so much!"

We took a moment and raised our glasses to my beloved aunt, who was so desperately missed.

Have I said how much I love these ladies?

With bright red lips, the only other makeup I had on was a little mascara on my eyes, I felt like I looked good.

My hairpiece, as with all our hairpieces, matched our dresses. Mine was a large mother of pearl comb with a beautiful bouquet of feathers that cascaded off the right side of the comb and curled around my ear.

I decided we were going to do something like this every single year. It was so magnificent. Every single detail so beautifully done, and I felt gorgeous (and slender) in my stunning gown.

In contrast to the ladies in our shimmering gowns, the extravagant decorations, and the twinkling lights all over the estate, the Macho Men looked all dark and broody decked out in their tuxes and black-tie.

It was a stunning affair.

After dinner and the MC was through praising all of the contributors, the party really got started with a hilarious bidding war over silent auction items. That wasn't all, we also had a full-blown auction. We had raffle prizes, and the raffle sales were being handled by flamboyantly dressed Carnival costumed individuals. There was a full band playing, and a dance floor that quickly became crowded, and a full hosted bar.

At some point before dinner, Lance found me and became the perfect escort. We danced; he pulled out every chair for me. He rose with me every single time I stood, and when I needed to excuse myself to go to the lady's room, he escorted me, waited for me outside the lady's room door, and then escorted me back to my chair.

Most of the Women of Wine Country was there, with the exception of Francesca. Her husband was still in hospice. I had actually only seen her away from his bed side once, and that was at the funeral, and I hadn't seen her away from her home where Frank was since.

The ladies did everything they could to support Francesca and the girls. Besides checking in on the small family regularly. A meal train was organized by the community, and the women made the deliveries so as not to disrupt what little time they had left with Frank. The ladies also made sure the girls were getting picked up and driven to appointments or errands. It was important that their needs were met during this horrible time in their lives. A time that was only going to get worse.

It's was what this group of women did for each other.

Lance and I were enjoying a wonderful conversation with one of Harmony Grove Municipal Advisory Council members. Lance was telling him all about his race cars. Apparently, Lance had been racing cars since he was a child with his uncle and could take a car apart and put it back together better than it was from the factory, (his words – not mine). One of the servers, who I didn't recognize, came to me and said I was needed back in the event hall kitchen. That was not my normal kitchen. Doug usually worked that kitchen and typically I stayed in the house kitchen and did my cooking there. But of course, if I was needed, I was

going. I excused myself the table and told Lance not to
worry, "I'll be right back."

I didn't want to interrupt him; he was in deep
conversation and everyone was having a great time. He
asked, "Are you sure Isabella? I don't mind escorting
you."

"No, it's fine, really. You've been such a great date; you
relax and enjoy yourself. I'll be right back. Whatever it is
it can't be very much. And shouldn't take but just a
minute."

I followed the server, who must have been with one
of the wineries; it wasn't unusual to have somebody I'd
never met before come up and ask me for something or
need me. We headed back towards the event hall, which
was all the way across the tasting room. We walked
through the busy event hall where all the booths were
set up and the information tables were and headed back
towards the kitchens.

Once we got to the kitchen, I realized there weren't
many people around and it was quieter than I had
assumed it would be. Dinner was done and all of the
dishes had been cleaned and cleared away. Most of the
service from this point forward would only happen after
the event was completely over and all of the guests and
vendors had left.

I slowed my pace and asked, "Where is everybody?
What's going on? And what could I possibly be needed
for back here?"

The hair on the back of my neck stood up as the server I was following turned around with a gun in his hand and said in a shaky voice, "I'm sorry ma'am, but I've got to take you now. Let's not make this hard. I need you to come with me, right now. I've got a car parked right out back." He indicated the back door off the kitchen.

I wasn't feeling great: a wave of nausea washed over me, and I broke out in a cold sweat. He wasn't coming across as the most confident bad guy I'd ever seen (not that I'd seen tons) but the few I had been exposed to recently were way more confident than this guy was.
"I'm not going with you!" I said.

He quickly became agitated, shoved the gun in my face, and shouted, "Go out the fucking back door and get in the goddamn car, or I'm shooting you!"

He thrust the gun at my face again, this time connecting with my cheek bone. It hurt and it scared the *bejeezos* outta me! I was getting sick and tired of this shit!

If he was going to shoot me, he was going to shoot me, whether I go with him or not. And the last bad guys were definitely trying to kill me. If I had my druthers, I'd rather die right here, than be somewhere else going through God knows what.

I screamed as loud, and as hard, as I could, and I kicked him with my pointy shoe. I kicked that guy as hard as I could and reached for the first thing I could find, which was a coffee urn that had been washed and set back up on the island. I grabbed it by the handle, swung with all my might and smacked him across the head with it.

Hard.

Hard as I could.

That made him twist sideways; the gun went off. It was loud. As in really freaking loud.

I ducked down behind the island and screamed again, just as Captain Steve, several of the Macho Men, and Lance, followed by a ton of other people, rushed into the kitchen.

They found me down on my haunches cowering behind the island.

"He tried to shoot me! I think he went out the back!" I shouted, pointing from my position behind the island. Several of the Macho Men took off out the back door.

Lance looked irritated and a little confused. Believe me I understood; I was confused too. I noticed he kept running his hands over his head making his hair stand up. It's weird the things you focus on when you're freaking out.

"Oh my God Isabella! Are you okay?" Captain Steve said, as he rushed to me and pulled me up from my cowering position into a big safe bear hug. "Goddammit Isabella, you can't be left alone for a second" he whispered to the top of my head.

Goddammit was right! Cabe was going to come back around when he heard about this.

That was the last thing I wanted!

CHAPTER 18

What's Love Got to do With It?

Just as I thought, Cabe came immediately. He had to have heard right away based on the fact that he was at the estate lickety-split.

I was sitting in the large living room of the house with the police and several of the Women of Wine Country, their dates, Lance, and Captain Steve, who was holding me in his big safe arms.

The party guests and servers were giving their statements to the police, which couldn't have been much 'cause nobody was there but me and the jerk who had tried to shoot me, or take me...make me go with him...whatever.

The police were all over the estate, and of course, I had a whole brigade of Macho Men hanging around when Cabe suddenly stormed through the door. He stopped to talk to Roman for a few minutes. During this conversation, his head swung, exorcist style, to me, and as soon as his eyes landed on mine, my stomach dropped, and I knew I was in for it.

At this point I would like to state how unfair it is how sexy Cabe Brown was. No amount of buttheadedness would ever deflect that fact.

His long, angry, aggressive stride brought him directly in front of me. If that wasn't enough, the look on his face said it all. He reached down, grabbed my upper arm and pulled me out of Captain Steve's hold, (note: Captain Steve did nothing to resist Cabe) and dragged me behind him as fast as I could walk in my heels, out of the room, down the hall, and into the bedroom on the first floor I was still occupying.

He kicked the door open, (yes kicked!) pulled me through the doorway and slammed the door shut behind us and threw the lock. Once inside, he released me and I began to back away from him. I wasn't scared of him, I knew he would never physically harm me, but I wasn't sure exactly what he had in store for me. I'd never seen him this mad, and I'd done a pretty good job of making him mad from time to time.

He stalked towards me. I backed up until I hit the wall. I had nowhere else to go, but he still came at me until he was directly in front of me, so close, I had to tilt my head up in order to look at his eyes; he was as close to me a person could be without touching.

He placed his hands against the wall on either side of my head, leaned in, "Goddammit Isabella! I can't leave you alone, not for one fucking second! You're already getting yourself in trouble. You're going to end up dead!" he growled at me. I could see he was visibly shaking, and it was having an effect on me.

He was freaked out!

His freaking out was freaking me out!

Why was he so upset? He chose to date someone else – making it clear I wasn't that important to him. What the heck was going on here?

He must have felt responsible for me because he was under some misguided belief Antonio left him to watch over me. That had to be it. Well, it was time to set him straight.

"Goddammit back to you Cabe! I didn't do this! They came *here*, even with all the Macho Men, all the security, even the Harmony Grove sheriff is here! How much more protection does a girl need, for heaven's sake!" I cried.

"Isabella." Cabe still growling, said back, like saying my name was an answer for something. Putting his weight on his hands, he leaned even closer, so close we were now touching chest to chest.

"You know, I didn't just run out of the house willy-nilly saying here I am shoot at me, shoot at me, shoot at me! And another thing, take a step back," I finished, on a shout.

Cabe stared at me for a few minutes and leaned back so we weren't touching anymore but didn't move his hands from either side of my head so he could be right back into my space anytime he wanted.

"Look, I told you that you're not to put your hands on me again. You don't get to march in here, grab me by the arm and drag me out of a room full of people. You lost any right you had to behave that way with me."

He straightened, put his hands in his pockets, and looked at the ground like he was trying to compose himself. I stood before him in my beautiful gown, shaking from an evening of terror and my newly formed anger.

Shortly after I delivered that little nugget to him, and he gave me space, we heard banging on the bedroom door and Lance yelling on the other side, "Isabella! Isabella, are you okay?"

Oh great! Lance had the worst timing.

Cabe looked up at me, his face going cold again, "Now you're dating the pretty boy?" He used his thumb to point over his shoulder towards the door.

"Let me in, Isabella!" Lance yelled, banging louder. "It shouldn't matter to you who I'm dating and who I'm not dating." My voice was shaking.

"Damn little help he's been. That pretty boy can't protect you."

Jumpin' Jezebels!

"I *am not* dating him. And even if I was, I wouldn't be dating him because he could protect me. You've got a whole slew of Macho Men to protect me. I don't need to date somebody to protect me, Cabe."

Cabe took a step back towards me. I could see how angry he was, and I wasn't sure exactly what he was angry about, except anger seemed to be his default emotion when it came to anything having to do with me these days. Was he frustrated that I was once again put in harm's way?

"Look, I don't know how much more security you're supposed to put around here, but you are the security guy, so maybe you need to step it up," I said, pointing my finger in his chest. I went on, "I thought you were the one who had security all figured out around here. This is your job, to protect me, all of the guests, and this winery. This is your responsibility and you're the one who fell down on the job this time. And speaking of that where were you tonight Cabe? Were you out with *Jennifer*?" This last statement was beneath me, and I knew it, but danggit it felt good to say.

Cabe's shoulders relaxed and he took a half a step towards me again, "Isabella'." he said softly.

"Oh, no you don't! NO! No Isabella! No soft, growly, sexy Cabe voice! There will be none of that!" I shouted at him.

Before he could respond, I lowered my voice and said, "Cabe, I know you think Antonio left you to watch over me like some old chauvinistic romance novel, but he didn't. He left you to make sure the winery wasn't run into the ground my first year. That's all."

He waited a second, then two and finally after what seemed like a year, he said, "Growly sexy Cabe voice?"

"None of that either!" I said and stomped my foot.

Cabe stepped back to me, pressing his whole body up against mine and said, "I fucked up Isabella. I know I did, and I'm sorry for hurting you. It was fucking stupid and I'm not stupid. If it matters, I took Jennifer home and left her there. I didn't want to be with her. I don't want to be with anyone... not anyone but you."

"Step back Cabe." I wedged my hands between us and pressed back on his stomach. He didn't move back but instead leaned in and rested his forehead against mine.

"I'm in fucking love with you Isabella." He whispered. "You make me crazy and sane all at the same time."

"What?" I breathed. "You hurt me Cabe. You hurt me, and you did it on purpose. I don't know how you expect me to get past that. I don't know if I can."

"Isabella, you have to. I need you. You make me want to be a better man. Being around you makes me a better man."

"This is you being a better man?" I asked, exasperated. I reached up and grabbed onto his forearms that were braced next to my head.

"Abso-fucking-lutley." His voice was the deepest I'd ever heard from him. He lifted his forehead from mine and kissed my temple softly.

After delivering that bomb, he turned on his heel and left the room. Lanced rushed in as soon as Cabe cleared the door frame.

That was such a bullshit move! Leaving me standing there, after that kind of bombshell on this awesome night (turned terrifying night) and now, confusing night!

Someone must have drugged me.

I wasn't sure if I'd imagined the whole thing.

I didn't know which way was up. I did know I wasn't going to be able to dissect this without the ladies' input and I was going to need it STAT!

Lance stood in front of me asking if I was okay and if he needed to do anything for me. I tried to stay focused on him but couldn't. I am not even a little ashamed to say I was super relieved when Captain Steve walked into the room, took my hand and gestured to the door. I looked at Lance, shrugged my shoulders and tucked myself under Captain Steve's arm. This was exactly where I felt safest.

Luckily for me, I missed the look that swept over Lance's face when I walked past him.

Captain Steve walked us back into the living room where all the Macho Men and some of the police were still hanging around.

"Isabella, I recently rescued two bullies from a shelter. I thought they might make good guard dogs because they're a bonded pair, and they work really well together. I've put them through extensive testing and their natural guarding instinct is high. But they are also used to living in a home with people and that may not make them the best choice to be perimeter guards. I want to bring them over tomorrow morning so you can meet them and see if they are a good fit for you. That work?" This was from one of my regular kitchen visitors, Marcus, aka Macho Man number two. I knew from our lunch time conversations he ran the K-9 division of the security company Cabe owned, SDI – Security Deployment International.

"Thank you, Marcus, that actually sounds like a great idea!" and it did. If the dogs liked me, and I liked them, they just might be exactly what I needed.

I looked around the room at the wine tribe who was hovering and said, "Ladies, we need to talk!"

"Finally!" Becca yelled.

******

Later that evening, Roman, Marcus and Cabe replayed the images of the fake server who tried to take Isabella. Every inch of the estate was under surveillance. They had already pulled the stills of the guys license plate. The car that had been outside the door, running and waiting – waiting until the driver heard the gunshot and took off. The images were circulated to every law enforcement agency in the area, as well as Cabe's security team.

"This guy wasn't a professional; he was terrified. In fact, I'm not sure who was more scared, Isabella or him." Roman commented. "The guy outside, however, drove off as soon as he heard the gun shot, as calm as could be." He said pointing at the monitoring screen. The car had been idling outside waiting to load Isabella up and take her off to God knows where.

"Isabella really clonked him hard, didn't she?" Cabe sounded a little amused and a lot proud.

"Yes, she did." Marcus responded, "Luckily."

"We have to find the server; he's going to be the weak link," Cabe said, looking at Marcus.

Roman put his hands on his hips and said, "You find the server, you bring him to the station, or better yet, call a car to come pick him up. I don't want you going rogue on me."

"Guess you'd better make sure we don't find him first," Cabe replied.

Roman looked at Cabe, then to Marcus. The men had known each other for several years and Roman didn't always approve or appreciate Cabe's interference. Especially when it came to Sydney and his relationship.

But he knew Cabe.

He knew Cabe's guys were very good at their job, Cabe was even better. Sometimes this was a big asset. Sometimes it ended up being a big nuisance.

"He pointed a gun at Isabella. He scared Isabella. No one does that and walks away." Cabe said.

This was going to fit in the nuisance category.

Roman smiled to himself. He was going to have to pay close attention to Cabe; nuisance or not, it was going to be fun watching him twist and turn. Because if Roman knew anything, he knew one thing; and that one thing was, you didn't fuck with a woman's emotions like Cabe did Isabella's and get off lightly.

No, Cabe was going to pay dearly. And Roman was going to have a front row seat to the whole show.

This was going to be fun.

CHAPTER 19

Jake and Annie

The next morning, true to his word, Marcus showed up with the most beautiful white bullies, I'd ever seen.

They looked like they were a cross between an American Bull Dog (huge) and a Pitt Bull (muscular). The male, Jake, was a giant snow-white guy with two little light brown spots on one ear. And the female was also snow-white and just a little smaller than her brother, with a light brown circle on her right eye. Her name was Annie. She looked very similar to the old Little Rascals' dog.

Once Marcus let them out of the back of his huge impressive kenneled truck, they stretched and sniffed around.

While they busied themselves with their sniffing around, I stood stock still. I was a little taken back by how big and scary they looked.

Marcus walked over to me and said, "Have you ever had dogs, Isabella?"

"Nope." I said, with a little pop sound on my "p".

"Are you okay with them so far? You look a little scared."

"Yep." I replied, with the same pop on my "p".

"Ok, Annie, Jake c'mere," Marcus yelled and let off a low whistle. Both dogs immediately turned and ambled their big bodies over to him.

"These two are super gentle. They honestly don't know they are any bigger than their heads. They have no clue they are big and scary. Isabella, I wouldn't bring you any dogs who wouldn't work for you. You trust me, right?"

I looked down at the two huge beautiful dogs who were waiting for whatever Marcus had called them over for, both of them were not only wagging their tails but also their entire back ends. It was freaking adorable.

I leaned down and reached out to the male, Giant Jake, and said, "I trust you completely." And scratched Giant Jake's head. Jake enjoyed having his head scratched so much, and he showed his appreciation by hauling his big body over to my legs and flopping down on my feet.

"How old are they?" I asked.

"We think they're about three," he replied.

"Who's the biggest baby?" I cooed to Giant Jake and scratched the top of his head. Looked at his sister, I cooed to her, "Are you my baby too? Huhn, are you? Are you?" She immediately came to me, and I scratched her head.

"Alright, I'm going to get their kennels set up for you on the balcony in the kitchen, so when you are working, they have somewhere near you to hangout. Your bedroom is where they will sleep. I have their beds. I'll put them in there, that's where I want them sleeping, not in bed with you. They need to be free to roam at all times. And I want them with you when you're up and around."

Still loving on the dogs and not even looking at Marcus I said to them, "Okay, that sounds great doesn't it my babies? Yes, it does! Yes, it does!"

I heard Marcus muttering about "ruining his guard dogs" or something like that, but I couldn't care less. These were the most adorable babies I'd ever seen, and they were going to be with me for as long as I could keep them.

It turns out whoever's dogs they were before they ended up at the Harmony Grove animal shelter had taken very good care of them. They knew several commands, were low energy and basically just wanted to lay around at my feet all day and get fed treats. They shadowed me everywhere I went.

I ended up having to buy, from Amazon, two large decorative kennels to go onto my balcony area off of the kitchen that they stayed in while I was in the kitchen cooking, so they wouldn't contaminate any of the food. As soon as the new kennels arrived, I had Marcus come pick up the ugly-as-sin-monstrosities he had originally set up for my babies.

Marcus and I did have a little bit of a heated discussion about the new kennels when he came to pick up the old ones. I showed him the new kennels and how pretty they were. The wood on the top was reclaimed barn wood and the bars were a gorgeous decorative cast iron. I paid a mint for them, but I was receiving a hefty paycheck with almost zero expenses, so I could afford to splurge, and they did not disappoint.

Anyway, Marcus thought I was ridiculous; I knew this because he looked at me crazy-like and said, "Cabe has lost his ever-loving mind! No wonder he's been a moody son-of-a-bitch!"

Whatever.

Anytime I left the kitchen area, or I wasn't standing and cooking they were at my feet. I couldn't make a move without them. I couldn't even go to the bathroom alone. They would sit and cry at the door until I opened it, and then they would both crowd inside the bathroom. It was kind of hilarious, and it was also very sweet, and thinking back, I was never actually alone again after welcoming those two sweet babies into my home.

I hadn't yet broken a few things to Marcus, who checked on the pups daily. First, they didn't sleep in their beds, they slept tucked into me in my bed at night.

Second, Marcus was never getting them back. After the comment about 'Cabe losing his mind', I didn't feel so bad about keeping them, or spoiling them. I was starting to feel safe and relaxed again. It was a really good way to feel and it was a gift these two sweet babies gave back to me. They deserved every treat I gave them.

He was right on one thing: these dogs had no idea they were supposed to be guard dogs. They thought they were sweet and lovable and that's how they acted. I'd never seen them in their big and bad mode until one afternoon, when some poor unsuspecting soul rang the door chimes and they went ballistic! It took me off guard how they responded, and I was a little apprehensive at first by how ferocious they looked.

It wasn't long before I got tired of the barking. I walked up behind them and said "Enough!" in a firm exasperated voice. They both instantly stopped and sat as much on my feet as they could, pressing the weight of their bodies against my legs.

Looking down at them, they did look ferocious with the stripe of guard hair standing up. The delivery guy who had rung the door chimes couldn't get out of there fast enough.

I loved them even more!

Cabe had been in and out and around the winery. When he heard Marcus brought me the dogs, he came in, met the pups, walked them around a little bit, gave them each a treat, decided they were perfect for me and left without ever saying a word directly to me.

I didn't say anything to him either. It was weird. I couldn't forget he had said he loved me, but I also couldn't forget how badly he had hurt me. I believed him when he said he took Jennifer home after the bar and didn't stay with her...but it still didn't change that he had made love to me the same morning he knew he was going to be going on a date with another woman. How was I supposed to get past that?

When he did check in on me, strangely, the pups wouldn't alert me when he came in. They alerted me for absolutely everyone else ... but not the one person I would have liked to know was coming.

Figured.

A few nights after I adopted Annie and Jake, Captain Steve came by to share dinner out on the balcony. Since we had an event that night, it was around nine pm before we were able to sit down and relax with our food.

My feet were hurting. I was experiencing swelling in my feet and ankles that I'd never had before, so it was new for me. Of course, being on my feet all day was fairly new for me too and I was keeping long hours. I attributed it to that and realized I was going to have to get a thick rubber mat or something to stand on while I was cooking and baking.

Luckily, my appetite had fully returned from my stomach bug and I was hungrier now than ever before, but I seemed to be losing weight still, my arms, my back, my stomach was smaller around my rib cage, even my thighs and bottom seem to be smaller. The only part of my body that wasn't getting smaller, were my boobs, which were heavy and sensitive.

After we finished eating dinner, and Annie and Jake realized no more table scraps were coming their way, they both slipped under the table and laid on my feet.

My feet were so sore, and it hurt so much I grimaced and moved my feet out from under them. Captain Steve saw what was happening and pulled my feet onto his lap.

"Isabella, your feet are so swollen," he commented, and all I could think was what a bittersweet moment, because it reminded me of the first time Cabe had done that after the funeral.

I didn't mention any of what I was thinking when Captain Steve proceeded to give me one of the best foot rubs I've ever had in my entire life, even better than the one I got from Cabe.

I let out a little whimper. It felt that good.

And yes, I did it even not having sex.

That of course, is when Cabe decided to burst in on our dinner. See, what'd I tell ya? Annie and Jake didn't even get up from under the table to alert us Cabe was coming in.

What the heck? Traitors.

I tried to drop my feet from Captain Steve's lap, but he held on tight, so I looked up to Cabe and said, "Do you need something?"

"I stopped in to check on you, Isabella, to see if you were okay. I guess I don't need to worry about you being okay, now do I, Hernandez?" Obviously, this was spoken to Captain Steve not me.

"Hey dude, you stepped away, so I stepped in," Captain Steve responded.

Holy heck!

"Wanna take your fucking hands off Isabella asshole?" Cabe said menacingly.

"This is the second time you've asked me to take my hands off Isabella. And this time, I'm thinking no. No, I wouldn't. I'm hanging on to her." And he pulled my feet closer to him, which actually hurt a little. I gritted my teeth and was not really paying attention to anything but my feet now being gripped tightly when I heard: "Mother Fucker!" Cabe growled and lunged at Steve, who must have known what was coming 'cause he suddenly threw my feet off of his lap and lunged back.

The two ridiculous men wrestled around on my balcony, knocking the table and chairs over, spilling the dishes and cutlery and forcing me to stand on my sore feet. Annie and Jake jumped up and barked at them. "Stop!" I screamed. But neither of the stupid Neanderthals were paying any attention to me. They were too consumed with their ridiculous egos.

It was utter chaos on the patio. The men had destroyed the table and broken dishes and food was strewn all over. The pups were freaking out and barking at the two ridiculous men who were hitting each other.

I was done.

I just wasn't up to this and these stupid childish men.

I called to Annie and Jake and once they came to me, I lead them off of the balcony, through the kitchen toward my bedroom when I felt an overwhelming wave of nausea wash over me. I took off running as fast as I could to the bathroom, where I barely made it before emptying my stomach in the commode.

I was starting to think something more was going on than the stomach flu. With that last thought, another wave of nausea washed over me and I ended up retching until my stomach had nothing left to give and still, I heaved.

I heard the door open but couldn't move my head to see who it was.

The faucet turned on and I heard water running, then I felt large familiar hands move my hair off of the back of my neck and a cool soothing washcloth was draped over it. Eventually, my stomach stopped heaving, allowing me to relax a little. I was partially lying on the floor, but I was too afraid to let go of the commode.

Strong arms scooped me up and carried me from the bathroom to the bed. I was so weak from vomiting I could barely hold on.

Cabe laid me on the bed and retrieved the washcloth from the bathroom and gently placed it on my forehead.

"Isabella, what's going on with you?" Cabe asked quietly, sitting next to me on the bed.

"I've been battling this stomach bug for a while now, but I thought I had it beat." I certainly wasn't going to share my suspicions with him yet.

"How long have you been throwing up?"

"This is round two. I had a reprieve for a few days but must have been reintroduced to the bug." I sure hoped he was buying this, and we weren't going to head into a very uncomfortable conversation. "I usually start feeling better pretty quickly after getting sick." And sure enough, I was already feeling better.

"Why did you come by tonight? And why would you start a fight with Captain Steve?" I asked, needing to shift the conversation away from me being sick.

He looked at the necklace I was wearing.

"You're wearing the necklace I gave you." He commented off topic. I touched the small pendant that sat at the base of my throat and said, "I never take it off. It comforts me and gives me strength. I touch it and I feel the love from Raquel and Antonio through it."

"I miss you Isabella. I needed to lay eyes on you. Every so often I come by to watch you cook," he said, answering my previous question.

What?

"What? When? Why?" I asked scooting myself up into a sitting position.

"Why?" Cabe looked at me and stretched his arm over me, placing his hand on the opposite side of my legs so he was leaning across me. "Because I fucked up Isabella. I don't like myself much because of it. You deserve someone better. But I can't get you outta my fucking head long enough to let that happen."

"Cabe..."

"You aren't like any woman I have ever met." I didn't know where this conversation was going, so I stayed quiet. "Everything just rolls off of you like water off a duck's back. Nothing rocks your boat. With all the bullshit thrown at you since Antonio passed, you adjust and move forward, without skipping a beat. Nothing phases you or slows you down."

That wasn't how I saw myself at all. And I was about to tell him that, when he went on to say, "I guess I shouldn't be surprised; it's gotta be from a lifetime of dealing with that crazy fucking mother of yours."

Do not ask me why, but my first instinct was to defend my momma. Yes, I agree, it was a stupid response, so I stayed quiet about it.

"Tell me you love me," he said quietly. "Tell me you love me just a little. Tell me I haven't fucked myself completely."

I wanted to tell him that I was so in love with him he stopped my heart from beating. But his previous actions, and my need for self-preservation kept me from speaking. I had too much at stake to give so much of myself away to him.

We sat there staring at each other when Jake howled at Cabe, drawing our attention to the pups and

Annie jumped on the bed, to get closer to me and snuggle her big girl body up against mine.

"Whatcha up to big guy?" Cabe asked Jake, who looked at him, howled again, and then he too jumped on the bed only to flop down as close to me as he could get, pressing his big soft body against mine opposite Annie.

I panicked, looked at Cabe and yelled, "Don't tell Marcus!"

Cabe threw his head back and roared with laughter.

Chapter 20

Tests

I sat staring at the pregnancy test I'd laid on the table in front of me, unable to believe the results I was seeing with my own eyes. While I knew it was coming, I knew I'd been unusually sick and nauseated, and then unusually hungry and had been losing weight, I still couldn't believe I was pregnant.

I wasn't supposed to be able to get pregnant. This was my aunt, my momma and my curse. My momma never really talked about it, but my aunt made sure I knew. My father left my mother because she had a very hard time conceiving, and when she was able to conceive, she couldn't carry to term. My father didn't know she was six weeks pregnant when he abandoned her. She never told him about me, ever. That's when her true bitterness set in; during the pregnancy it took hold.

Two years after I was born, she found out my father had married again and had another baby.

But here I was, looking at a positive pregnancy test. Pregnant.

I was pregnant with Cabe Brown's child.

Now what the heck was I going to do? Not only was I stuck with him at the winery and in the ownership of the winery, but now I was stuck with sharing a child with him? I wondered how much time I had before I wouldn't be able to hide it and he'd find out, if he didn't already suspect.

I'd ordered the pregnancy test online so no one would know about it. I wasn't leaving the estate alone at all after that last attempt on my life, and I didn't trust people not to talk if I asked them to buy me a pregnancy test.

The info was just too juicy to expect people to keep to themselves.

I didn't really know who I could actually trust, I mean, I knew all of the Women of Wine tribe were there for me, and I knew without them I wouldn't be able to do this.

But I also knew they would get together and decide what was best for me concerning Cabe. I wanted to decide what was best for me concerning Cabe.

With them, I was strong enough and had enough friendships, community and family that I could raise a child on my own. I knew without a shadow of a doubt, they would support me and become this child's family.

But I wasn't ready to deal with all of that yet, and I wasn't ready to let any of them know either, especially after the last time I tried to talk to them as a group; none of them agreed on anything! It was a fiasco! Individually, they gave great advice; as a group they disagreed and started arguing with each other, which did me no good at all.

My first instinct was to call Sydney and tell her, but I wasn't sure if she would be able to keep it from Cabe. I knew she wouldn't do it to betray me, but she might think she knew what was best for me, like the other ladies, better than what I knew was best for me, and that just wasn't the case.

Yes, things were getting better with Cabe and I. He had started coming in occasionally to eat lunch or would show up in time for dinner.

Apparently, during the time I thought he wasn't around, he had been coming by and watching me without me knowing it. That in itself was kind of weird, but also, I kind of liked it. Maybe I was a little twisted, but even though he hurt me, and I knew he was capable of doing it again, I wanted him. I wanted to be with him, and I wanted to be happy.

Yes, he'd told me he loved me. But I didn't trust that love. Was is solid or was it full of holes? I wasn't prepared to put all my emotional eggs back into the Cabe basket just yet.

What I didn't want was for him to be with me only because I was pregnant, so I wasn't ready for him to know yet.

I'm not sure what made me do it other than a lifetime of this being the only person I had around me on a daily basis, and she would be the only living person to know what huge news me being pregnant was. I picked up my phone and stared at it for a while, before making up my mind and texted my momma.

All I said was, "Momma, are you ok? I need to see you. I'm pregnant."

I waited for the response, and when one didn't come, I decided I might as well put the pregnancy test away and get on with my day.

I had three events that evening and the days following, several more. I was trying to keep myself as busy as possible. Cabe's recent bizarre behavior, and the fight he had with Captain Steve had thrown me for a loop. I wasn't sure what to make of it and I'd enough going on, that if I stayed busy enough, hopefully I wouldn't dwell on it.

Stacy popped in and pulled me out of my kitchen and into a meeting about the winery to learn how well we did, and about the weight of grapes that were brought in from harvest. Stacy was a bundle of energy and was looking forward to giving the feedback on the events. We were booked out through the rest of the year. We were more worried about double bookings than anything else.

Looks like we were going to have one of the largest years that we've ever had with the grapes; it seemed that my aunt and uncle's hard work was paying off and this is going to be one of the better years Bellini Estates had ever seen. Even the fire didn't set us back.

I wish I could have told Antonio how well his vines had done this year. He would have been so proud.

I made it through the meetings in a stupor, not really hearing everything, but just sort of taking it all in. All of the data was given to me on paper, so I would be able to go over it all later. I smiled and nodded and asked (what I hoped were) correct questions. Knowing that everything was okay and there weren't any disasters that we had to take care of made it better.

I was walking around like a zombie, so I decided the safest, most productive place for me was also my favorite place in the world, my kitchen. I headed back to my beautiful gleaming kitchen to finish the baking for the events coming up.

I was in the kitchen watching a Facebook live of one of my favorite sommeliers learning more about the different types of wine, when a text message came through on my phone and it was from momma.

"Oh baby that's wonderful news we need to celebrate! Can you come see me right now?"

That was weird. I don't think she had called me baby in decades or written out a whole word since she started texting. And wonderful news? Maybe things were turning around with her.

I replied I wouldn't be able to come right then but that I did want to see her. Was it possible for her to come to the winery?

I really didn't think it was safe for me to leave and I certainly wasn't willing to take any chances at this point. I had more to worry about than just me.

She sent a text back right away saying yes that she would meet me down by the river at two o'clock. That gave me just over an hour and a half to get my baking to a point where I could put it to rest for a bit, while I went and met momma. I text her back and told her *'Bring your appetite and I'll pack us a lunch'*. We could have a nice late lunch down by the river together.

I was so happy I was going to be seeing her. I knew she was a nightmare, but let's face it, she was my nightmare and I would always worry about her. This is the longest we had gone without communicating, even in the past when she was nasty, at least I knew she wasn't in the hospital or jail...or worse.

Eventually everybody would know that I had met my momma 'cause every inch of this winery, estate and vineyard were under surveillance by Cabe and his gang of Macho Men, but that's okay. She's my momma and when everybody finds out why I was meeting her, it wasn't going to be an issue. If it was, they would all have to get over it.

I finished up all the baking and prepared a light lunch of cheese and bread and some fruit for momma. I grabbed a couple bottles of water, and because momma wasn't a big animal person, put Annie and Jake in their kennels with a couple of beef rib bones and headed down to the river.

I saw somebody down there waiting, but I couldn't make out who it was. As I got closer, I saw that it was not my momma, but Mark. Well at least I knew it wasn't going to be long before everybody came running. As soon as somebody saw that he was on our property, all of the security forces were going to converge on us.

"What are you doing here Mark?" I asked, "Where is my momma?" I stopped far enough away from him that I could high tail it outta there if he made a move towards me.

"Hi Isabella," He said looking down at my stomach in such a manner I felt threatened. Every protective instinct in my body had me placing my free arm over my stomach.

"Your mom asked me to come get you and take you to her. She wasn't feeling very well, and she wasn't able to get out of bed today."

"What are you talking about? Is she okay? What's wrong with her?" I asked.

"What isn't wrong with her?" He sneered, "She's nothing but a disgusting drunk."

"Well then, why are you with her? Oh, don't bother. Let me guess, you're with her because you really wanted the estate. You never ever planned on being with her long-term; you just wanted to get ownership of Bellini Estate and Antonio's grapes."

"You think you're so smart, don't you?" He said stepping closer to me.

"That's all you ever wanted from the beginning. Guess what? We know all about you, Mark. We know that you killed my aunt and my uncle."

"You stupid fucking cow, you don't know anything. You don't know what you're talking about!" He was so upset; spittle flew with each word he spoke.

"I know you're doing this for the Markins; they wanted my uncle's grapes!" When I shared this bit of information, he went still and said, "Who else knows girl?"

"Everybody, Sydney, Cabe, all of the Macho Men, everybody knows. It's not a secret and detective Roman knows too."

"That's too bad for you, but really good for me. Come on. You're coming with me." With that, he pulled out a gun and pointed directly at my stomach, saying,

"I'll shoot you right in the stomach so even if you manage to survive a gunshot wound…. your baby won't."

"Please. Please don't shoot me." I seized with panic dropped the basket with the lunch I'd prepared in it,

and wrapped both arms around my midsection.

"Come on, my car is parked around the corner. Let's go"

I could only pray that somebody was watching the monitors.

*****

Lucas was monitoring the Bellini Estate, along with several other high security risk establishments, from headquarters at SDI. Some were clients, a few were under investigation by their team, and a couple were personal projects one or more of the team members were working on.

He'd just taken a bite of his calzone when he noticed that weasel Sephos drive onto the estate, prompting him to switch screens to where Isabella was marching out the back door and heading directly to where Sephos was now waiting.

"Motherf...." he mumbled, as he picked up his cell and dialed Cabe.

"Yeah." Cabe's standard answer.

"Man, your *Chica* is meeting that fucking weasel Sephos now, at the estate."

"She inside or out of the house?"

"She's heading down to the river where Sephos is currently. Looks like he is waiting. He's pacing and acting shifty. I don't like it man."

"Fuck!" Cabe yelled. "I am too far away to get there quickly. Call in Roman and see how far out he is. Of all the fucking days to have called everyone off on other assignments!"

"We gotta work man. This isn't your fault."

"You say that again to me if anything happens to Isabella."

"Okay. Okay. I get ya."

"I'm on my fucking way."

"You got a locked on her?"

"Yeah, I just brought her up."

"Drive like a bat out of hell man! Sephos just pulled a gun and is aiming it at her midsection."

"FUCK!" Lucas heard Cabe shout as the call ended.

CHAPTER 21

Bella Baby

Mark took me to an abandoned harvesting shed outside of town. Once inside, it took my eyes a bit to adjust and when they did, I could see my momma laying on a filthy mattress with a chain locked around her ankle and attached to a pole.

The old harvester shed was a large metal building, with a concrete floor that was all busted up. There were huge chunks of concrete, debris and rebar everywhere.

I stumbled a few times and had to be careful where I stepped. It looked like lightning had struck and left big holes everywhere in the concrete floor.

The smell of the old abandoned shed was so nauseating; it was all I could do to keep from gagging. I wouldn't be able to hold the contents of my stomach down for long. I could feel the hot saliva building up in my mouth and I was going to have to concentrate to keep myself from retching.

The sight of my momma, dirty laying on the disgusting mattress, with her filth all around her (they hadn't even given her anything to use the bathroom in) sickened me further. You could tell she had been there for a while. Her hair was matted and sticking out in every direction. It looked like she was in the same clothes she'd worn to court; it was hard to tell through the filth, but I was thinking that was the truth. She was clearly drugged; she wasn't drunk and passed out like I've seen her hundreds of times before.

My God. What had he done to her?

Yes, she was a mean drunk.

Yes, she needed to get it together and clean up her act. Yes, she had been awful to me most of my life. But this was my momma, and no one had the right to treat her this way. She was chained up like a dog, one I'd try to rescue from its horrible living conditions.

"What have you done?" I asked, turning to look at Mark.

"What? She deserved it. Your mother is nothing but a drunk. I couldn't stand one more day with her. I only needed to keep her to lure you out. Once the judge dismissed the contested case, I had very little use for her, and I couldn't stand her anymore." Mark sneered at me.

"What do you possibly think this is going to get you? I can't sign the winery over to you. Sydney and

Cabe have measures in place to keep that from happening. If you kill me, my momma will not inherit the winery. Sydney will remain the executor and Cabe will inherit my portion of the estate; that's the way my aunt and uncle wrote it up." This was looking worse and worse. Once he realized he'd backed himself into a corner, who knew what he would do.

"That's too bad. I guess I'll be keeping you alive and using your mother to keep you in line. I had planned on getting rid of her, but maybe she will come in handy after all."

"Do you honestly think you're going to keep me, and my momma, contained for over a year? While I'm pregnant with Cabe's child? You honestly think that's gonna work and that Cabe is just gonna to give up?"

I heard a car as it pulled up outside and prayed that was my rescue team. I wasn't feeling super good about it however, 'cause if I could hear the car, so could Mark and he wasn't looking worried. In fact, he looked smug.

"Just you hold on now Isabella, I've had a little bit of help. Why don't you meet my partner?"

The door opened to the harvester shed letting the sun stream in and in walked Lance Drake.

"Help! Lance!" I yelled, "Mark is holding us! Run! Get help! He has a gun!" I screamed.

Lance didn't run. He didn't freak out. And he wasn't scared of the gun.

"Okay Isabella, just hang on now, let me talk to Mark and figure this all out." Lance responded, walking towards us, like this was a normal dispute and he just needed to hear the other guys side.

A cold dread washed over me. "What exactly are you doing here Lance?"

Ignoring me, Lance turned to Mark and said,

"What the fuck man?"

"I told you I was bringing her here."

"Yeah, you did, but you didn't bother to talk to me about it first! You've completely fucked us good now. I was getting somewhere with Isabella. We were finally dating."

"We weren't dating." I muttered. I was so shocked that Lance was standing here talking to Mark while he was holding a gun on me, and my momma was chained to a pole while laying on a horrid mattress. I was having a hard time wrapping my head around this entire situation.

"You stupid imbecile! You've ruined everything! You've ruined all my hard work. Everything down the drain. She's seen me. You purposely let her see me! You were supposed to protect my identity. What the fuck man?" Lance was losing his cool and I hadn't ever seen him this disheveled before. He kept running his hands over his head and was making his hair stand up. It was weird; this was the second time I focused on him doing this while freaking out.

"You weren't going to have anything to work on as soon as Cabe finds out Isabella is pregnant with his fucking kid."

Lance slowly turned his head to look at me and screamed, "You stupid fucking whore! I went through all that trouble to get rid of Antonio and Raquel. You were never supposed to meet Cabe or Steve. You should've fallen for me; I could've married you. At least it would have lasted a year or two before I completely took over the vineyard and winery."

"My God I'm gonna be sick." I mumbled. And I was. I could feel it building up. "This is crazy. I can't believe any of this is happening. Lance, how could you? I thought we were friends!"

"Really?" He laughed but it looked more like a snarl, "You thought somebody like me could be friends with some southern hick like you?"

At his words I started crying, realizing how completely stupid I was. How was I so totally fooled by him? "Come on Isabella, no hard feelings; it's just business."

I'm not sure how everything could've gone so terribly wrong or how we possibly ended up in this situation, but I knew my child had to be protected first and foremost.

And nobody chains my bitch ass momma to a freaking pole!

"Were you behind the men in the SUV attempt to kill me? And the gun man at the Gala?"

"Those stupid assholes. The Markins thought they could scare you into selling or letting your mother take over. I knew it wouldn't work and when they realized the will excluded your mother from inheriting, and then they lost the lawsuit contesting the will, they completely pulled off the project." Lance said coldly.

Jumpin' Jezebels!

I'm glad at least my instincts were honed well enough that I was never really interested in this creep. What could I have ever seen in him anyway? Looking at him now, all I could see was a skinny blond wimp.

"That's when he and I joined teams. I had already put in so much time with your mother I wasn't willing to walk away with nothing. She made it impossible to walk away with nothing. Having to deal with her was fucking horrible," Mark filled in. Like some bad movie, these two were going over their whole plan with me, which told me they never expected me to make it out of there alive to tell anyone the story. They planned to kill both me and my momma.

"You can't be so foolish to think that Cabe is just going to go away." I was reaching for straws, and I knew it, but I had to try to get us out of this and I was starting to worry if that was going to happen.

"It doesn't matter!" Lance was really agitated now and was going nuts on his hair, running his hands through it over and over, making it stand straight up, in every which way, like some mad scientist.

"You've seen me! You know I'm involved, and you know I was behind the accident that killed Raquel and Antonio!"

I was going to vomit any minute. I kept talking trying to buy myself some time. I chanced a glance at my momma laying on that awful mattress and noted she hadn't moved once since we entered the shed.

Looking back to Lance, I whispered, "Why?" Tears streaming down my face; I was totally freaking out, but also trying to buy time. I didn't know if Cabe and his band of Macho Men, or Roman and the police knew where we were, or if any of them would reach us in time to rescue us.

Lance looked to Mark and said, "We need to get rid of them. We need to do it in a manner where they can't be found. Do we have any hog farms around here?"

"Yes, but I think it'd be quicker with less chance of being caught if we weighted their bodies down and sunk them in the river. Not the Mokelumne, but the American."

"Are you seriously discussing how to get rid of me and my momma's bodies right in front of me?"

Lance walked to me and said, "Come on, enough chatting. Let's go."

I looked at my poor momma and couldn't stand to see her like that one moment longer.

"I'm not going anywhere until you unchain her. She's been treated like an animal, worse than an animal. I'm not doing anything until you free her. How do I know she is even still alive?"

Lance looked over at her and then told Mark, "She's so high on devil's breath, she isn't going to go anywhere or do anything. Unchain her; she's like a fucking zombie anyway."

I watched as Mark walked over and kicked at my momma's prone body. When she didn't move, he set about unchaining her leg from the pole.

Suddenly, my momma was up and moving at a pace I'd never seen her move at before. And then my momma did something I never realized she was capable of. She picked up a piece of jagged concrete the size of a bowling ball and slammed it against the side of Mark's head. Once, twice and then he toppled over while he was still holding the gun. His head made a sickening sound as it hit hard on the concrete. The gun skidding across the floor. The sound of the attack echoed off the metal walls. Then she lifted that chunk of concrete and brought it down on his head again, and she did it again, lifted up above her head and came down, this time with an animal screech. Each time the concrete piece struck his head it made a distinctive wet crunching sound.

As soon as I registered what was happening, I noticed Lance too, was registering what was going on. Before he could make a move, I squatted to the ground, reached out, grabbed hold of the first thing I could, popped back up with a large piece of rebar that had a sharp bent end on it and I swung with everything in me.

I swung that piece of metal at his head for my unborn child. I swung again for my momma, who was dirtier than she'd ever been her entire life and chained to a pole. I swung that rebar at his head for my aunt, for my uncle, and for all of the horrible things these two people had done.

I swung, and I swung, and I swung, and even after he was on the ground, I kept swinging.

Before I was done my face was covered with brain matter, skin, blood and all sorts of other lovely bits and pieces of Lance. I had completely obliterated his face, and by the end I was swinging blindly. Once I used up all my strength, and knew he wasn't ever getting up again, I fell to my knees and finally allowed myself the luxury of vomiting.... everywhere.

And when I say everywhere, I mean everywhere; on me, on Lances still body, the concrete - everywhere.

By the time Cabe, his band of Macho Men, and Roman with the police, finally came through the door, that's how they found us. What a site we must have been. I was on my knees, covered in vomit, blood and bits of Lance's head. Momma was still beating Mark's head in with the chunk of concrete she'd found and screeching in a way I would never forget.

I could feel Cabe standing over me.

I dropped the rebar with a loud clatter, wiped my eyes with the back of my hand, and looked up at him. I watched Cabe's eyes move from me to Lance and so I looked at him too. It was impossible to make out any of his facial features.

I'd seen to that.

I looked over at my momma when I heard her cry and rail out a horrific scream. Seems she wasn't ready to stop beating Mark over the head with her concrete weapon and didn't take kindly to having her weapon taken away from her.

I looked back up at Cabe, who hadn't moved.

"Holy shit Isabella." Cabe whispered.

"I'm okay. Check on my momma, I don't think she's gonna recover from this Cabe."

"I don't give one fuck about your mother." Cabe dropped to the ground next to me.

"Careful Cabe, you're going to get goo on you," I tried to tell him as he wrapped his arms around me and pulled me to him. "Oh well, now you've done it. You have all sorts of nasty stuff on you."

We heard someone yell "Heads up" and then I was suddenly knocked back from a side tackle. It was my momma and she was chanting over and over, "Bella Baby. Bella Baby. Bella Baby." She curled up to me and laid her cheek against my stomach and slid to the floor, still chanting "Bella Baby. Bella Baby. Bella Baby."

Cabe let me go and I curled over my momma and whispered "You're okay now momma. Everything is going to be okay."

She looked up into my face, her eyes wild and crazed, "We're gonna have a baby!" She screeched.

Jumpin' Jezebels!

CHAPTER 22

Two Heartbeats

Cabe, his band of Macho Men, Roman, the police, an ambulance, a fire engine (with Captain Steve) and a news crew were all bustling around the harvester shed, a harvester shed I never wanted to see again for the rest of my life.

Ever.

While the Macho Men crew kept the news reporters and cameramen back, the EMT's, with the help of the police officers, peeled my momma off of me. But if she was forced more than a few feet from me she became enraged, and I would have to calm her back down.

Therefore, I stayed with her while the firefighters tried to clean us both up, and the EMT's worked on Lance and Mark. They eventually sedated momma enough they were able to get her strapped to a gurney and hauled off to the hospital where she would spend the next few days, and many more in recovery and therapy. God willing, she would be able to keep her sobriety up. This was the first time she was even willing to give it a try.

Cabe and I got in a huge argument about whether I needed to go to the hospital or not. I said no, he said yes. Everyone in earshot voiced their opinion, and none of them were on my side.

He won, but don't think for one second, I didn't store it away for future weaponry, especially since there wasn't anything wrong with me. I tried to tell him that, but I guess when someone you care about is covered in human goo; it tends to freak you out a little.

I knew he really cared about me, 'cause he was totally freaked out. I knew this for a fact, 'cause he wouldn't let me go, even when the EMT's made their way to me to assess my condition.

Between him and momma, I was starting to need a little bit of my own personal space back.

From there it only got worse. The wine tribe arrived at the scene and started carrying on like I'd never seen them do before!

Jumpin' Jezebels!

There was wailing (Terra and Jenna) and cursing (Becca) and fussing over me like I was a toddler just pulled from a deep abandoned well (Sydney and Stella). The only one who made any real sense was Jules, who saw that I was okay and went directly to Roman and the other police officers and ripped into them like none of us had ever known she was capable of.

The police and Roman were shocked and looked a little frightened.

It seems when Jules is scared for someone, she's grown to care about, Mama Bear comes out and she has claws, teeth and one heck of a mouth on her!

Everyone quieted down (all except Becca, who kept right on cursing) as they brought the bodies out on stretchers.

Mark had no pulse. My momma had taken care of him but good. He was covered up completely, so we all knew he was gone.

Lance had a pulse that was weak and inconsistent; they didn't think he would make it, but had tried to save him.

I didn't feel one bit bad.

Not one. He was going to kill my baby, my momma, me... and wanted to feed us to hogs!

I turned away so I wouldn't have to see his beaten in head and face as they rolled him by us. Becca said in an uncharacteristically low voice, "Damn it, Cabe, you beat the shit outta him!"

"Wasn't me," Cabe responded in a similarly low voice, and looked down at me - making the ladies look at me with a mixture of horror, curiosity and pride (that last look was from Becca).

"He wanted to feed me to hogs!" I yelled to the group. "Can we get to the hospital already?" Geez.

Finally, after what seemed like hours at the hospital of me recounting what happened to what seemed like five-hundred-million police officers and detectives, we were able to ditch the wine tribe, and made it back to the estate. I only wanted two things: One, to take a shower and wash the grime of this horrible day off of me, and two, my sweet little fur babies.

I went straight to the shower. I stood under the scalding water and it felt so damn good to wash what was left of the disgusting blood, vomit and pieces of Lance off of me once and for all. Good riddance.

I stood in the shower with the spray beating down over my body and watched as the goo slid down my legs, across the tile, and circled the drain before disappearing in a surreal colorful daze.

Flashes of the day filled my head and I knew at some point I was going to need to talk to someone about everything that had happened since arriving at the estate. But that could wait.

Before hitting the shower, I'd asked Cabe to ask one of his guys to let the pups out once I was in the shower. I didn't want them to see me this way. I told him where their treats were, so hopefully they wouldn't have any issues.

After the most divine shower of my entire life, I patted myself dry, slipped into my big, fluffy robe, pinned my wet messy hair to the top of my head and left the bathroom.

I found my pups on my bed waiting for me. I honesty had never been so happy to see anything in my whole life as I was to see those sweet babies right then.

Maybe I was being a little over dramatic, but I deserved it after everything I'd been through.

I laid down and curled my body around Annie, and Jake lay in the crook of my bent legs, resting his big heavy head on my hip. It felt glorious. Annie curled up against the front of me and my big gentle giant at my back was the safest I'd felt all day. Maybe these two were going to be all the therapy I'd need. One could hope.

"You do realize Marcus is going to want the dogs back now that you and your mom slaughtered the bad guys." Cabe was standing in the doorway watching us.

"Over my dead body." I mumbled. Cabe hadn't brought up my momma's outbursts and I was hoping he would let it go and act like he hadn't heard it.

"I have to admit I'll feel a lot better on the nights I have to work out of town with them here."

"Whatever." I muttered and cuddled further into my babies. No one was taking them from me.

"We need to expose the dogs to children so we know how they will act before the baby comes."

My eyes popped open. I was facing the opposite direction so he couldn't see my face. Then I had a thought. Yes, I was reaching, but I'd do anything to get out of this conversation.

"How'd you guys find me?"

"What?"

I rolled my upper body over without disturbing Jake and flung my free arm out across the bed. "Did you

guys track Lance? Did you suspect him all along? How
did you find us?"

Cabe watched me a beat, leaned his shoulder
against the door jam and said, "This is what we're going
to talk about?"

I nodded yes.

"Okay fine, we'll do this your way. I put a tracker in
your necklace."

Jumpin' Jezebels!

I stared at him for a beat. "What?" I yelled, not really
sure if I was mad or just surprised.

I then whispered, "Thank God." and rolled my upper
body back to once again snuggle Annie. I settled on
surprised.

"Not that you needed it."

I rolled my upper body back so I could see him,
flopping my arm out across the bed again.

"What's that supposed to mean?" I asked.

"You'd already saved yourself by the time we got
there. If I wasn't so fucking freaked out by all that
happened, I'd laugh. Those guys never stood a chance
against you and your crazy fucking mother."

I was speechless. Didn't he realize they were gonna
kill us? This wasn't funny!

I squinted at him.

But I couldn't get too mad; he didn't know how me
being pregnant was a big deal. Only momma and I knew.
Only I knew how she would kill anyone who tried to

hurt this baby. I knew it with my whole being. But there was no way Cabe would know.

He must have seen the look on my face 'cause he went on to say, "That was their first and fatal error: thinking they could control your mother. All over some fucking awards."

"What awards?"

"The Markins may have backed out when things got dicey, but they knew full well that Lance had tampered with Antonio and Raquel's car. All of this was over their award-winning wines they couldn't make without Antonio's vintage Cinsault grapes. According to the info Sydney and the ladies dug up, they were going to lose a couple of their biggest accounts if they didn't continue to win awards. Awards they knew they were going to lose without Antonio's fruit. Lance was trying to get control for his family so they would have a chance at the accounts."

"These must have been some pretty big accounts for all this trouble."

"Millions."

"Wow. So, have they been arrested?"

"No. No proof, it's all speculation."

"WHAT!" I sat up, dislodging Jake's big head. "What is stopping them from coming after me again?"

"Me."

"They still came after me before, when you were here." I said.

"That was Lance and Mark. Also, you weren't my wife and the mother of my child then." He went on, "Besides, I'd feel sorry for anyone who tries to fuck with you or our baby after what I saw you did to Lance."

"Don't remind me." I said laying back down to cuddle my babies. I knew I was going to have nightmares over what I'd had to do to Lance.

"You are the most badass woman I know." He said quietly to my back.

"You're crazy." I mumbled. But I was starting to feel a little warm flush come over me. Did he really think I was badass?

"I'm not the one cuddled up to a couple of giant pit bull guard dogs and calling them 'my babies'. It took three of my guys to get them out of their kennels, and if Marcus hadn't shown up, my men would have gotten their asses handed to them."

I snuggled deeper into my sweet babies and cooed loving nonsense at them.

"Isabella, nothing rocks you; you roll with the punches better than anyone I've ever seen. Even when you're knocked on your ass, you get up stronger, fucking prettier, and more capable than before. You can bend a man to your will with your food and your beauty - but the best part is, you have not one fucking clue you're doing it."

His voice had gotten closer while he was talking, so I wasn't surprised when I felt the bed compress as he sat down next to me.

"You're the only woman I have ever met who is soft enough to interest me, but strong enough to withstand me. I won't be able to walk all over you. My work won't scare you, and my guys already love you. I can't stop thinking about you and I don't even want to. I'm in so fucking deep with you Isabella, I need you. Marry me Bella."

My stomach fluttered. He wanted me to marry him! He loved me! And he called me Bella!

"You just want to marry me because I'm pregnant."

"No. I want to marry you *now* because you're pregnant. I knew I wanted to marry you the day of the funeral when I had my hands wrapped around your beautiful feet and you moaned. Be my wife Isabella."

I flushed. Shoot. I did do that.

"I am not putting up with any of your passive aggressive bullshit where you decide to push me away by dating someone else."

"I regret doing that to you Isabella. More than you'll ever know."

"Yeah well, I marry you, that means you're mine; you do that shit again and you'll think Lance got off easy." I wasn't kidding. I'd hurt him.

"Strongest fucking woman I know." He mumbled as he snuggled up to me, Jake and Annie.

"You're going to have to stop saying fuck. At least around the baby."

******

The wedding was held at the winery two months after Isabella and her mother stopped the two men that kidnapped them both and tried to kill them. Lance succumbed to his injuries the day after he was taken to the hospital. His family was furious, and everyone knew it wasn't over. Now, not only did Cabe and Isabella have to worry about the Markins, the Vista Rio family was gunning for the newlyweds too.

For now, they would celebrate and enjoy life. A new life and a new beginning.

Isabella wanted to have the wedding as quickly as possible, not wanting to walk down the aisle with an "even bigger buddha belly" than the one she thought she had.

The wedding was simple and sweet, and she wore a cream-colored gauzy dress Jenna had made for her. The beautiful dress was floor length, with spaghetti straps and no adornments. Isabella wanted everything simple and easy. Cabe wore a pair of gray slacks and a white untucked button up shirt with his sleeves rolled up. Isabella's bouquet and decorations were a variety of wildflowers with no order to them. All that mattered to her was that they were colorful.

The Women of Wine Country tribe, Sydney and her girls, and the Macho Men group were the only ones in attendance except employees, who were more like family anyway, and the Italian aunts and uncles.

The ceremony was simple and sweet. The couple didn't have anyone stand up for them. They didn't need anyone but themselves and they knew it.

A giant Scot with a thick accent, who'd recently joined Cabe's team, hilariously officiated.

The reception was a simple family style dinner, with everyone pitching in. Isabella stood off to the side and watched as her mother set one of the dishes down on the long table and went back in for another dish to bring out.

This was going to be a long road for her, but she was willing to do anything, she said, to be a part of Isabella's, Cabe's and the baby's lives.

Cabe made it clear to Cynthia, any abusive language or action and she would be cut from their lives, regardless if she was sober or not.

Only time would tell if she would be able to keep it up. They had never been through anything like this before and she hadn't had a drop of alcohol since – so maybe.

She glanced over to the grassy area where Annie and Jake were playing with the children. They were some of the employees' kids who were always at the estate. It would be a good life growing up here.

They had started calling Annie "The Nanny" due to her gentle nature and care of any child who visited.

Jake was an adventure dog all the way and would fetch anything thrown for him. Bringing it back was another matter entirely, and he made a game of having the children chase him to retrieve whatever it was to be thrown again.

The children loved the dogs. They were so sweet, gentle and so very happy.

Isabella laid her hand across her belly; tonight, she would let Cabe know that the doctor heard two heartbeats at the appointment she'd had earlier that week. She wasn't sure which news was scarier to deliver – the two heartbeats or that Isabella had a doctor's appointment without telling him.

Only her mother understood why she needed to have that first visit alone. Tonight, Cabe would know too.

Touching the pendant at her throat brought up the feelings of love... and loss. She knew how happy her aunt and uncle would be to see the estate alive with the celebrations and the sounds of the children's laughter.

It was bittersweet knowing without their deaths, Cabe and Isabella wouldn't be celebrating their special day or the new innocent lives they were bringing into the world.

It was time.

Leaving the party, she went into the library and retrieved the envelope she'd placed in the desk drawer so many months ago.

Isabella sat down and began reading.

EPILOGUE

My Dearest Isabella,

First, I love you.

I've loved you since the idea of you came into being. I wish you had been born to me instead of Cynthia. My sister didn't deserve you but needed you so desperately I never had the heart, or courage, to try to take you from her.

My beautiful strong Isabella, you always put yourself after everyone else. You are amazingly strong and resilient. You have to know by now what a blessing you are to not only your mother, but to all of us. You are the light in our family.

You and I are very much alike. We love and care for those around us. We fight for what's right and we don't give up. We hurt easily, but we also forgive easily. This is our gift, but also our curse.

However, you are also your own person. You are brilliant, kind and compassionate. I fear it will be easy for you to get trapped into other people's problems.

Try to protect yourself, Isabella. It's important you're able to realize your full potential, and I worry that the weight of others might keep you from the opportunities you deserve.

Find someone to love Isabella. Get married. Have a family and enjoy your life. It's much shorter than any of us realize.

I am so sad I won't be there to see the amazing woman

you will become, to share in your marriage, the births of the children I pray you are able to conceive, and all of the success life has to offer you.

If by chance, my beloved Isabella, you find yourself unable to have your own children, please don't follow my footsteps. Trust me when I tell you it's a lonely life without little ones. Adopt, Isabella. Fill your home with beautiful children. Fill your life with love and laughter, fights and tears: just fill it.

The one real regret I have in life is not sharing our lovely home with babies. Antonio would have been so much happier with me if we had. And I would be leaving him with a family of our very own instead of alone. This is my one biggest regret.

When you do fill your home with these beautiful souls, tell them about me.

Please don't let me be forgotten. Encourage Antonio to share stories of his wife with your children, so I do not fade away as if I'd never lived.

Teach your children my recipes. Teach them to make my lemon cake for Easter, my red velvet for Christmas, and my pecan pie for Thanksgiving.

Hopefully, every holiday you'll share stories of me with the children and keep my memory alive a little longer.

The thought that I might be gone and forgotten is the burden I carry for wasting time and not getting around to adopting children of my own. Don't remind Antonio; he was never happy with me that I put off filling our home with children until it was too late.

As I write this, I already mourn the idea I won't be around to hear the laughter of your children fill my quiet halls. I take comfort knowing Antonio will be there to enjoy them as they play and grow.

You are all I have, so the heavy weight of keeping my memory alive falls to you and Antonio.

A few things I'd like to share with you I never got a chance to:

Decide what you want and go after it. Do not let me, your mother or anyone else stop you.

Fall in love Isabella. You will never regret it. When you do fall in love – love fully. Pride and insecurities stop most of us from loving passionately – don't let that happen to you. When you find that man who does it for you – love him every single minute, of every single hour, of every single day for the rest of your life.

And lastly, choose your battles wisely. You can't die on every hill Isabella; make sure you only fight for what really matters.

I am so sorry, my beautiful Bella, I am not there for you. I know this time will be hard, but know with every cell in your body, that I love you more than any other human on this earth next to my Antonio. You, Isabella, are the last of my blood.

My friends will hold you up and help you with Antonio; you can lean on them, Isabella. They will love and protect you with every breath in their bodies – these women I leave you with, shall be your strength and salvation - this I know from the depths of my soul.

Even without the children, with a quiet empty home, I have a beautiful life full of love, laughter and success. My beautiful Isabella, please don't mourn me, but instead celebrate the amazing life I lived. When you think of me, remember my laughter and my pleasures. Remember, I found the love of my life, my beautiful Bella, and I know how special that alone is, for so many never do.

Please take care of your uncle. He will be lost without me. Make sure he eats and takes his medicine - he will forget. My Antonio is a strong loving man, but he has his weaknesses and his biggest is me. Without me, I don't know what he will do, and I don't want him to stop enjoying his life. Make sure he doesn't withdraw into himself as he can sometimes. It's not healthy for him.

I know I ask so much of you, but he is my life, my love and all I hold dear.

The two of you are my whole heart.

With these last words I leave you until we are joined again, all my everlasting love,

Aunt Raquel Bellini

The Women of Wine Country Series has just begun!

Want more fun and excitement?

Watch for these titles releasing soon;

Lawyer & Liar – Sydney and Roman

Beauty & Betrayal – Jenna and Marcus

Want to stay current on all the shenanigans? Sign up for our email list at womenofwinecountry.com

> Follow us on Facebook Women of Wine Country group and like us on Facebook: @WomenofWineCountry Page for apparel and events in the Lodi Wine Appellation. And @authorwellsbrown for updates on the new series T Wells Brown is working on.
> Instagram @womenofwinecountry and @twellsbrown
> Pinterest: Women of Wine Country
> Twitter @twellsbrown
> Podcast Women of Wine Country on Apple, Stitcher, Spotify and all supporting PODCAST platforms

Thanks for reading!

Please add a short review on Amazon and let me know what you thought!

The Author

Casey Evans Photography

www.womenofwinecountry.com

A Note from the Author

Usually this is where you'd see an author bio. A little blurb about the person whose imagination sparked a story, and whose diligent work created a book you'd (hopefully) want to read.

Since it's typically the author writing their own bio it felt somewhat disconnected to me, so I thought I'd just give you, the reader, a little informal information about me and the rest, if you're still interested, can be found on all of my online and numerous social media platforms.

I am Yaya to three beautiful little ginger Diva's that are featured (as grown up's) in my books. I will let you try to guess who they are.

The two dogs you see in my author picture are the real-life Annie the nanny and Jake my beloved gentle giant. I wrote them as they truly are. Both of them were rescued from a shelter many years ago and they have been a blessing for my husband and myself. I couldn't imagine my life without them.

We have two additional rescues; they are featured in later books so unless you follow me on social media, you'll have to wait for the books they are in to meet them.

I live in the Lodi Wine Appellation and there are many descriptions in the books that are accurate. If you find yourself in our neck of the woods, you'd be able to see landmarks or recognize roads I've written about.

While Bellini Estate is completely fictional many aspects of the estate have been taken from several different wineries in the area. If you do make it to our wonderful wine region; there are many resources available to you and if you join the Women of Wine Country Facebook group, we could get those resources to you.

I am devoted to animal rescue and a portion of the sale of every book goes to help support shelters, rescues and resources benefiting the homeless pet population.

I have three grown sons who I cherish, but who will probably never read any of my books (this series anyway).

The Man of My Dreams is my beloved husband of almost thirty years. He came to me as a bodyguard and we fell in love instantly. This man is as Alpha as they come and supports me and all of my endeavours one hundred percent. How an old school Alpha male, and a small bossy woman manage to make it work after all these years is beyond me, but it does work for us. And I am thankful for my life with him.

I like animals' way more than people, and I like people a heck of a lot.

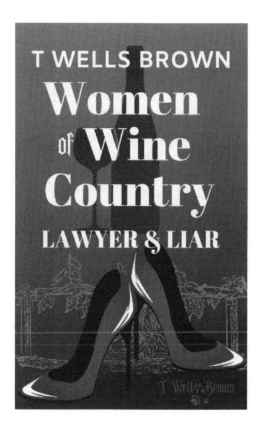

Sydney never planned to spend her life running from the Russian Mafia. But that is exactly where she finds herself after she stumbles upon an officer involved shooting late one-night. Will she be forced to leave her Wine Tribe in order to keep them safe? Did the officer survive the shooting? Will she survive herself? You don't want to miss Sydney's story! Releasing Fall 2019!